# "DON'T DO THIS," SAID SLOCUM.

They lifted him on his roan and pulled it to the nearby oak tree. Joady threw the rope over a thick branch while Ketchum held the roan.

Slocum felt the cord around his neck pulled tight. Suddenly he realized his number was up. These crazy bastards were going to string him up and didn't care if he was the right man or not. Rage scorched his body, but he couldn't do a thing; his hands were tied tight, his neck was in a noose, and in the next minute he'd be dancing on air...

# OTHER BOOKS BY JAKE LOGAN

# JAKE LOGAN

## SLOCUM AND
## THE NOOSE OF HELL

BERKLEY BOOKS, NEW YORK

SLOCUM AND THE NOOSE OF HELL

A Berkley Book/published by arrangement with
the author

PRINTING HISTORY
Berkley edition/May 1986

ISBN: 0-425-08773-5

A BERKLEY BOOK ® TM 757,375
Berkley Books are published by The Berkley Publishing Group,
200 Madison Avenue, New York, N.Y. 10016.
The name "BERKLEY" and the stylized "B" with design are trademarks
belonging to Berkley Publishing Corporation.

PRINTED IN THE UNITED STATES OF AMERICA

# 1

The sky blazed red and orange when the three men on black horses came out of the high coppery brush and rode toward Slocum. He was at his campfire, sipping coffee and admiring the low-brim forked green hat he'd picked up at the river crossing.

Slocum studied the riders, his senses alert, as they always were when he saw strangers on the trail. One man, sturdy and strong-jawed, wore a marshal's badge; the other two were lean, taut, and dark-eyed. The marshal smiled as they swung off their horses.

"Howdy," he said. "We're looking for a gunman, tall stretch of a man name of Dustin. His trail went near here. Happen to see him, mister?"

"No," Slocum said pleasantly, standing. "Didn't see anyone."

"Dustin shot Hank Jones and his brother, Lem, then rode south in a hurry toward the Sierras. Thought we might head him off."

The men stood around, casually bringing out smokes.

Slocum stroked his chin. "Wish I could help you, Marshal, but I haven't seen a thing. Been mighty quiet round here."

The marshal struck a match to his cigarillo. "Itchin' to hang a man like that."

One of the deputies who had edged to the side of Slocum said evenly, "Why don't we hang this man instead, Marshal?"

Slocum, who didn't like the joke, didn't like a stranger sliding beyond his vision, went for his holster, but the deputy had a derringer already sprung from his sleeve.

"Just raise your hands, mister. I'll take the gun."

Slocum's hands went up slowly, his eyes narrowed.

The deputy pulled the Colt and threw it far into the bushes.

Within two minutes they had his hands tied and a rope around his neck. Slocum fixed a hard eye on the marshal. "What the hell is this?"

"Looks like a hanging, mister," the marshal said pleasantly. "There's a good tree, Joady," he said to the lean, high-cheekboned man who had lifted Slocum's gun. "Get his horse, Ketchum," he said to the other man.

"Hanging? What the hell for?" Slocum demanded.

The marshal puffed his cigarillo. "Pick a reason, any reason. How 'bout horse theft?"

"That's my horse," Slocum said grimly.

"What's the difference? You could be a horse thief,"

said Joady, grinning. "C'mon, Floyd, let's get it over with. We ain't got much time."

Slocum stared at Floyd. "You're a marshal like I'm a horse thief. You're making a bad mistake."

Floyd stroked his chin, looking hard at Slocum.

"What are you waitin' for?" growled Joady. "We gotta move."

"Better make sure," said Ketchum.

Slocum gazed at him. "You got the right idea. Don't make a mistake in something like this."

Joady gritted his teeth. "It's him, it's him. We ain't got time."

Then Floyd made a decision. "Mebbe so and mebbe no. But we're taking no chances. Set him on his horse."

"Don't do this," said Slocum.

They lifted him on his roan and pulled it to the nearby oak tree. Joady threw the rope over a thick branch while Ketchum held the roan.

Slocum felt the cord around his neck pulled tight. Suddenly he realized his number was up. These crazy bastards were going to string him up, and they didn't care if he was the right man or not. Rage scorched his body, but he couldn't do a thing; his hands were tied tight, his neck was in a noose, and in the next minute he'd be dancing in mid-air.

He took a deep breath and stiffened his body as Ketchum struck the roan, which plunged forward. Slocum felt himself jerked off the saddle. The rope burned his neck and there was an intolerable choking sensation. Then he heard the crack of a rifle shot. The rope split and Slocum fell to the earth, gasping for breath. The three men ducked and started frantically to shoot toward the trees as they crawled to their horses, while rifle bullets made near hits.

Face down on the earth, Slocum heard the shots and the thunder of hooves.

He took a slow, deep breath.

He was still alive, though his throat hurt like hell. It had been something of a miracle; he'd never been that close to a hanging. He owed his life to the rifleman who'd done the shooting, a real marksman.

He heard footsteps and struggled to sit up to look at his benefactor.

It was not a man but a woman. She was dressed in a denim shirt and Levi's and carrying a rifle pointed directly at him.

Slocum gritted his teeth; this was a real bad day.

He studied her face. There was not much to be seen under the short-brimmed black hat and red neckerchief. But she got more interesting as she came closer: clear skin, deep brown, penetrating eyes, a finely honed face, thin eyebrows, a delicate, well-shaped nose.

Her expression was not friendly, nor was her tone of voice.

"I saved your life, mister, for one reason. That hat you were wearing. How'd you come by it?"

Slocum was a bit stunned. He'd got the hat ten miles back off a dead red-headed cowboy. The cowboy had been ambushed by Apaches. Slocum buried the man, and kept the hat since he'd lost his own in a sudden wind during the river crossing.

"Well?" Her voice was harsh.

He spoke slowly. "Apaches got this red-headed cowboy. He put up a good fight against three. He shot one, but they got him. Saw the tracks near the river crossing, where I lost my own hat. I buried him. Figured he wouldn't need his hat any more. That's how I have it, miss."

She gazed at him mournfully, then sat down on a nearby boulder. She looked hard hit.

His throat ached and he wanted in the worst way to get his hands untied, but the woman seemed deep in grief, so he waited.

Her eyes were moist and she wiped them with her red neckerchief. After a time, he said, "Miss, I know you're not feeling too good, but could you take a minute to cut this rope?"

Her eyes were clouded. "Who are you?"

"Name's John Slocum, and I was headed for Tucson before this unpleasantness."

"And where are you headed for now?"

His green eyes glittered icily. "Now I'm headed after three rotten hyenas who just tried to lynch me."

"John Slocum," she said thoughtfully and studied him. Then she came close, pulled a bowie from its holster at her hip, and slashed the ropes.

He felt a surge of relief as he loosened the noose and rubbed the skin of his neck, which felt raw and bruised. He rubbed his wrists to circulate the blood.

"Another thirty seconds, I'd've been swinging dead in the wind," he said. "Owe you my life, miss."

He walked to the bushes, found his gun, and stuck it in his holster. Then he went to the roan and pulled a pint of whiskey from the saddle. He took a long pull. When he came back, she was still on the boulder, her mouth tight.

"This man the Apache killed, was he kin to you, miss?"

"My name's Diana Keating. He was my cousin, Jake Kelly. He was helping me."

"Helping you?" Slocum gazed at her. "Helping you do what?"

Her mouth was a hard line. "Track those polecats."

He stroked his chin. "Why d'you spose they wanted to string me up?"

Her deep brown eyes stared straight at him. "That green hat. They never got a close look at Jake and figured you might be him. Didn't know Jake, just his green hat. I reckon they didn't take any chances."

Slocum swore softly. These hyenas didn't know for sure if they had the right man and decided it didn't matter, they'd swing him anyway. They had to be the mangiest men he'd ever met. His jaw tightened. He looked at Diana Keating. A good-looking missy, and she was hurting bad.

"They probably figured," she said, "that if they put out Jake I'd give up the chase. I can't track too good."

"But you're a dead shot, Miss Diana," he said gratefully, rubbing the raw skin of his neck.

She bit her lip. "I can shoot all right."

"Want some of this whiskey?"

"Wouldn't mind, Slocum. I can use it right now."

Slocum poured whiskey into a tin cup and watched her sip it. Then he thought of the men who, for no real reason, were ready to launch him into eternity. He felt scorched by rage, and had an overpowering desire to get on their tracks and pay them off. This woman also seemed interested in hunting them. He wondered why.

"Did you say you were tracking this marshal and his men, miss?"

"Marshal." Her lips curled in scorn. "His name is Floyd Mercer. He's a marshal like I'm Doc Holliday. He's traveling with his brother Joady and his cousin Ketchum. Three stinkin' hyenas." She drank more whiskey, which seemed to help her master her grief.

"I reckon they've done you some hurt, Miss Diana."

"They've done that, Slocum." She gazed at him, calmer now, then her face hardened, as if she'd made a decision about him.

"I told you, I'm Diana Keating. Me and my sister Belle own the Bar M ranch in Pima. My father died recently. Those three men were on our ranch for a month, and I made a bad mistake about them." She looked off with slitted eyes. "One night Joady got drunk, grabbed Belle, and spirited her off. Then Floyd, that phony marshal, figuring the jig was up, stole ten thousand dollars outa my safe and took off with him, joined by their cousin, Ketchum."

She stopped and looked at the high brush land where the trail climbed up and out of sight. "Probably had Belle back there with them. Kept her tied, I reckon, while they came down here, thinking you were Jake, to finish you off."

Slocum stared up the trail. She was a rich ranchwoman who'd lost a sister and ten thousand dollars to a bunch of dogs. She'd been hunting them with her cousin, who had the misfortune to run into Apaches. Now she was alone, and though she was a deadeye marksman, what chance did she have against three ornery dogs like them?

Still, she had guts. He liked that.

"Miss Diana," he said slowly, "even if you hadn't told me what these polecats did to you, I already decided to hunt them down and pay them off for trying to string me up. I owe you my life. Nothing would give me more pleasure than to team up with you. We'll go after your sister and your money, and try to pay off these men in blood."

She glowed as she looked at this tall, lean, powerful man with his strong-jawed, sun-bronzed face and steady green eyes. "I figured you to be that kind of man, Slocum. I'd thank you for your help."

Slocum nodded, pleased at her words. He gazed thoughtfully at the trail the men had taken. "They've gone through Apache country and outlaw country—bad little towns. We won't be able to call on help, just our guns. Not going to be easy, miss. Goin' to be rough times, I reckon."

Her jaw firmed. "I don't care. All I want is to catch up with them. I want Belle back. She's too young; she's reckless." Diana paused and a strange, hard glitter came to her eyes. "And I want most to get Floyd in the sight of my gun."

Slocum wouldn't mind that himself. But Floyd looked the most dangerous—shrewd, crafty, quick. She seemed to feel poisonous about him.

"Why do you want him that bad, Miss Diana?"

"I've got reasons, Slocum." Her voice was hard as nails. "I'd just as soon start after them now."

He smiled. "Exactly what I'm feeling."

● ● ●

They talked little, following the tracks until they came to thick brush country and steeply rising hills. In the distance he could see the purple peaks of the mountain pointing at the sky.

He liked her riding style—easy, straight, graceful. She had the tracker's instinct; her head moved often to scan the land. The threat of ambush could lurk behind any brush or boulder.

A slithering movement caught his eye, but it was a coyote on a desperate search for a jackrabbit. The breeze carried the sound of a sudden scramble as the coyote trapped its prey. Slocum's keen green eyes studied the earth, reading the meaning of the tracks.

The July sun was a ball of fire and waves of heat hit the earth. Slocum loosened his collar. Then suddenly he felt the skin on his neck bristle. He had just glimpsed the prints of two unshod ponies moving out of the brush toward the rise. Swiftly he scanned the land, then swung off his horse to look closely at the prints. They were fresh. Diana, startled, brought out her gun, although she saw nothing threatening.

"What is it, Slocum?"

"Apaches. The two who killed your cousin."

Her eyes slitted, but for a few moments she said nothing.

"I don't think they're too near. We wouldn't have birds for company," he said.

Her jaw was hard. "They killed Cousin Jake. A straight cowboy with a big heart. He dropped everything to come help me in my time of trouble. I loved him." She paused. "Can we do something?"

Slocum pushed his hat back on his head. So that was the man he'd buried at the crossing. He was no longer a dead body, but someone real, someone the lady cared about. He'd come to her help and got himself killed. Slocum looked at Diana and almost smiled. She was all guts. She could shoot and ride and seemed to have little fear. Yet the Apache was a powerful warrior. Even the other tribes feared them. Their ways of revenge could be terrible. Slocum's instinct was not to tangle with them, but he figured the Apache with his great tracking skill already had to know of the presence of the paleface and the woman. Revenge on the white man's woman was particularly satisfying to the Apache.

Slocum stroked his chin. Their trails had entangled: it was an act of fate. There was no escape.

"We have two choices, Diana. Run for it. But they'd pick us up when it was right for them. Or we could track them. That might give us the edge."

She looked thoughtfully at the hilly rise.

"I keep thinking they killed Cousin Jake. And I loved him."

He shrugged. "Well, if the worst happens, you won't get Belle back. And won't pay off Floyd Mercer."

She looked troubled. "Yes, that would be a great pity. But, as you put it, even if we decided to let the Apache go, *they* wouldn't let *us* go. I reckon we have no choice. And I'm thinking that Jake would be alive today if he hadn't come with me."

Slocum nodded, then examined the prints closely. Less than an hour old. The Apaches had gone up this rise, heavy with brush. They had lost a comrade. They felt rage for the white man, the land thief, the buffalo killer.

They had to be lurking. His jaw set.

Staying in front of her, he started up the trail, his eyes restlessly searching every possible site of ambush. Halfway up, he dismounted, pulled his gun, and motioned for Diana to stay put. He crawled to the rocky edge and slowly looked over. There, to his shock, was a grinning, red-faced, black-haired Apache, his knife in hand ready to throw. Slocum's instinct worked faster than his thought and his gun exploded, the bullet striking the Apache's chest, tearing a hole big as a fist. He hurtled back, and his body twisted in a spasm, but he was already dead.

Slocum, after shooting, had flung himself down, aware there had to be another Apache nearby. Swiftly, he crawled to his left then peered cautiously over the rise. The land was flat, with low grass, some cottonwoods, but no second Apache. Just the dead one, flat on his back, staring sightlessly at the sky. Nothing else anywhere. A mystery. Perhaps he'd gone back to the tribe, leaving this one to do the dirty work.

Slocum came down to where Diana was standing, her gun out. She had tethered the horses and crawled low toward the crest of the hill, hoping to help.

"We can ride now," Slocum said.

"I heard only one shot," she said.

He shrugged. "There was only one Apache. The other's gone. Back to the tribe, maybe. He's not hanging around."

Her lips were tight. "I want to look."

He watched her climb to the top and stare for several moments at the dead Apache. When she came back, her face was calm. "I feel better now about Jake." As they swung over the horses, she said, "I'm glad we didn't get into a long trackdown. There's poison in my blood. It won't come out till I catch up with Floyd and his rotten playmates."

The tracks of four horses—the three men and the girl, Belle—went toward the town of Cody. Slocum judged from the prints that they had about a three hour lead and were moving fast.

Because of the gruelling heat and the burden on the horses, Slocum stopped whenever he could to rest and water the animals. When the sun started down in a flame-colored sky, Slocum made camp near a small creek. They ate beef jerky, beans, and corn bread and drank coffee.

He thought of Joady, the brother of Floyd, and how fast he'd been about the idea of lynching. He remembered Joady's high-cheekboned face with its wicked brown eyes, sharp nose, and the scar at the corner of his mouth. It had been Joady, too, who during a drunk grabbed the girl, Belle. How could Diana have hired a hyena like that?

"This Joady—" Slocum began.

She looked at him sharply.

"He sure was in a sweat to hang me."

"The lowest breed of man," she said.

"How could you make a mistake about a man like that? Hire him, I mean."

"Well, Slocum, it didn't show right off. Came out when he was drinking. Anyway, I didn't hire him. It was Floyd Mercer I hired. He vouched for the other two. His brother, he said, would be a good man to have around, and his cousin."

"Good men for what—thieving?"

She stared off at the darkening sky. "I was deceived, Slocum. I thought Floyd was a good man." She paused. "I reckon you, too, were deceived by Floyd."

It was true. He had figured Floyd was a marshal. What kind of a man would dare put on a marshal's badge? The man had to be an outlaw to pull a stunt like that. Shrewd, too. It was that badge that brought down Slocum's guard, let Joady get the edge, and put Slocum within an inch of hanging. Yes, he had been deceived. You couldn't let a thing like that happen more than once. A slight misstep out here meant death.

"How'd they get Belle away?" he asked.

Her face hardened. "Belle's a dumb kid. Just hit sixteen and her blood's boilin'. She liked Joady. Didn't know he was a rotten dog. She may have been pulled out, but she was half willing."

"And what about this Floyd?"

"Floyd's the smart one. I gotta admit he's got a lot of appeal. I thought him straight and strong, someone to lean on." She paused. "Rotten to the core. I owe him a bullet in the heart."

Slocum's face was grim. "We'll sweat them a bit tomorrow."

He pulled the saddles off the horses, picketed them in good grazing ground, then set up his bedroll ten yards from hers, next to a fallen log.

He lay back on the bedroll, hands behind his head, and watched the big silver stars pop out of the dark blue. A great golden moon was low in the sky.

Lying there, Slocum relived again the moment when he felt the strangling of the rope round his neck. He thought of the three men. They were ready to hang someone, not caring if he was the right man. They had rustled off a young girl, stolen big money from the woman who gave them a job.

The rage that swept over him left him squirming on the bedroll. He would have hunted these men to the bitter end even if Diana had no grievance against them. The earth would be better off without them.

From the tracks, he figured they were headed for Cody where they'd pick up provisions, drink whiskey at the saloon, on their way somewhere.

He suddenly thought of the way Diana had looked when he asked her why she wanted Floyd that bad. "I got reasons," she had said, and the way she said it made him smile. It was easy to think of women as soft and cuddly, but some women, if crossed, could be tigers. Like this one. She could shoot like a demon. And she was one damned good-looking woman.

Not far away a coyote sent up a mournful howl. An answering howl drifted on the breeze from rocks nearby. There was a sudden flutter of wings as an owl dived on a squirming marmot.

The moon kept climbing, a big, full, and still golden moon. Through slitted eyes, he could see the nighttime silhouette of trees, the jagged edge of the mountain.

From where she sat on her bedroll, it seemed in the silence that he could almost hear her breathing.

Diana Keating. She'd saved his life. A beautiful woman. He had better be careful or he might get foolish about her.

Though the tracking was easy, they didn't reach Cody until noon. It was a typical town in the Arizona Territory, with a hot dusty main street, and lines of wooden houses that included a hotel, saloon, livery, and merchandise store.

They stopped at Johnson's Livery. Diana's big black had a loose shoe. The blacksmith, a stalwart man with light blue eyes and a short beard, had been hammering at the anvil. "Slocum's the name. We need a new front shoe for the black, Mr. Johnson."

Johnson nodded, turned to look at the roan, and smiled. The roan was a magnificent animal. Slocum liked to see him admired. He pulled out a dollar. "I'm looking for four riders, three men and a girl. Seen anything of them, Mr. Johnson?"

Johnson's blue eyes glittered as he took the money. "They stopped here. The girl's horse, a bay, needed a shoe."

"The girl. Everything all right with her?" Diana's voice was casual.

The smithy looked at the hammer in his hand. "Nice-looking filly. Looked a bit like you."

Slocum felt something odd in his tone. Diana flashed Slocum a sharp look.

"These men still in town, Johnson?"

"Been gone hours." A grim smile came to his face. "Some fracas in the saloon. Don't know much about it."

"Was the girl all right?" Slocum stared hard at him.

Johnson nodded. "Yes. She was okay. But there was a shooting. The men. Best you go there, get it from the horse's mouth. I don't mix into these things."

In the harsh sunlight, Slocum turned to Diana. "Johnson has to work on the horses. Why don't you go to the store, get provisions, then go to the hotel, take a bath.

You'll feel better. I'll find out what happened in the saloon."

She didn't like it. "All right. But let me know quick, if anything's wrong. I mean it, Slocum."

He started up the street, his boots kicking dust from the parched earth.

# 2

Burke's Saloon had a long bar, two card tables with players, a couple of women, and a stairway to upstairs rooms. The barman, a sour-faced man with a heavy head of curly black hair, came over. "What'll it be?"

"Whiskey."

He put a bottle and a glass in front of Slocum and studied him from washed-out gray eyes.

"The name's Slocum. I'm looking for Floyd Mercer. Seen him?"

Burke shrugged. "Everyone's looking for someone. Can't keep touch with 'em all." He leaned forward. "My job is to sell whiskey. I just do that, mister. Keeps my nose clean. You unnerstand."

Slocum scowled. There were always those who were willing to let evil men flourish because they wanted to keep their noses clean. Understandable; nobody wanted to die before his time. He shrugged, poured a whiskey, and gulped it.

"A drink for Marie, cowboy?" said a soft voice.

The girl came from behind him, smiling. She was dark-eyed, full-lipped, full-breasted, and wore a pink dress.

He poured whiskey from the bottle to the glass she held out.

"Just ride into town?" she asked.

He leaned toward her and spoke low. "I'm looking for a party of four, three men and a woman. Happen to see them?"

She looked at him with worldy-wise eyes. "See no evil, speak no evil, come to no evil." She sipped her glass with a slow smile.

He gazed at the creamy skin of her breasts, thrusting hard against the seams of her dress. With a jolt, he realized he felt his desire rising. He hadn't had a woman for some time, riding on the trail. And though Diana made his flesh tingle, he couldn't allow himself to make a try for her. She was a woman with troubles and, more than that, she had saved his life. You didn't tackle a woman who did that. Oh, he had powerful urges about her, but he bottled them. He gazed at Marie, at her slender waist and burgeoning hips, and the lusts of his flesh came intensely alive. It would be smart, he figured, to unleash his fleshly desires on Marie. In that way, he could keep firm control of himself in dealing with Diana. He was there to help Diana, not to seduce her.

Marie had been watching him and, with the experience of a woman who knew instantly when a man was primed with passion, she put her soft hand on his arm.

"Let's go to a place where we can talk, Slocum." And she moved her mouth suggestively.

Slocum felt a jump in his breeches. He put a dollar on the bar and the bottle under his arm. "Lead on, little lady."

As they went up the stairs, he figured that he'd have a quick game, so as not to keep Diana in a fret. He figured on finding out something about Floyd when he got this girl alone.

He scarcely glanced at the other men in the saloon as he climbed the stairs. The movement of her rounded buttocks kept his eyes riveted. There was a corridor and three rooms. She led him to the last which had a dresser, a mirror, a pitcher of water, and a bed with a yellow coverlet.

He put the whiskey bottle on the table, grabbed her, and pulled down on her dress so that her big shapely breasts jumped into view. They looked tempting, with big pink nipples. He bent down and lashed one with his tongue while his hands caressed her firm buttocks.

She laughed. "You're in a real sweat, Slocum, aren't you?" Her hand went over his buttoned excitement and her eyes grew saucer-wide. "Big man," she sighed.

He reached for the bottle, took a swig, put it back on the table, and began to peel off his clothes. She stripped quickly, too, fired by the promise of sex with this lean cowboy whose virility promised a good time.

Her dark eyes gleamed at the sight of his maleness, fierce and pulsating. Without a moment's pause, she dropped to her knees and began to caress it, first with her hands, then with her lips. Her mouth loved him as she

cupped him, and he was seeing stars. Fearful that he'd
finish that way, he pulled away. She stood up, smiling.
She had milk-white skin, a flat stomach, rounded hips
and thighs. His fingers reached between them into her
moist warmth and he stroked her. She began to groan
and her body coiled with passion. She reached out, and
he leaned over her body and went into her slowly. She
was tight and, as he went deeper, she sighed with pleasure.

His body moved slowly and she took his rhythm. His
hands caressed her breasts, her waist, her buttocks, while
he kept up a relentless rhythm. As he increased the pace,
his pleasure sharpened. Then his thrusts became harder
and fiercer. Grabbing her buttocks with powerful fingers,
he lifted her body to meet his thrusts until he felt the
climbing tension, a great swelling, then explosion. Her
body made wicked, greedy thrusts as if she had to have
every bit of him. Then she fell back on the bed in ex-
haustion.

After a while, she said, "Let's do it again, Slocum."

He laughed. "Love to, but I've gotta go."

"They don't come like you too much, Slocum."

He shrugged and they dressed. He put money on the
table.

"It's on the house," she said.

"Take the money." He lit a havana. "Floyd Mercer.
I'm looking for him."

"Yes, I heard you downstairs."

"What do you know, Marie?"

She walked to the window. Clearly she wasn't finding
it easy to tell him what she knew. It was probably out

of fear of Floyd. In truth, there was something sinister
about Floyd, a man who'd kill as easily as light a cigar.
Would Marie talk? She'd been softened up by the sex,
and he was hoping.

"They had a girl with them," she said finally. She
turned to look at him. "One of our boys, Amos Withers,
said it was a shame to bring a young filly like that into
the saloon. Joady shot Amos, just like that. Nobody
stepped in." She smiled grimly. "Not as long as Willie
James was standing by."

Slocum stared. "Who?"

She smiled knowingly. "Willie James. Sometimes he
calls himself Floyd Mercer, but back in Kansas he was
Willie James. Headed the Willie James bunch outa Dodge
City."

Slocum gritted his teeth. *Willie James!* Gang leader,
bank robber, train robber. Slocum remembered the posse
of long riders who came hard after the gang and broke
it. So Willie James had gone underground in Texas, sur-
faced in Arizona as Floyd Mercer working for the rich
ranchwoman, Diana Keating, to make a stab at respect-
ability, maybe. But Joady jinxed the plan when, in a
drunken fit, he grabbed the young girl, Belle. Then Willie
figured the game was up; he raided the safe and went on
the run with Joady, the girl, and cousin Ketchum.

What did it mean? Just that the man Slocum was
hunting was no ordinary lowdown thief, but a big-time,
deadly gang leader. Not a man who'd think twice about
hanging the wrong man. And Joady was cut from the
same cloth. What about Ketchum? One of the gang,
probably ready for desperate deeds. So what he thought

might be the pursuit of three ornery hyenas had become a deadlier trackdown. They were clever and desperate men with hellish experience.

Well, it might make the hunt a bit harder. But, Slocum thought, it took one bullet to finish a man, and it didn't matter how dangerous he was. The trick always was to get *your* bullet on its way before *he* got his.

Marie stood at the door, smiling, and he couldn't help thinking that bed was the best way to charm information out of a woman.

Nobody seemed to pay any attention as they went downstairs except the staring cowboy at the bar. He had a broad-boned face, a gash of a mouth, and deep-pitted blue eyes. He wore a black hat, a blue neckerchief, and a black leather vest. Slocum, alert to anyone who stared at him, noted the flushed face and twist of his mouth as it moved into something like a smile.

"Been lookin' for you, Marie," he said.

"Been busy, Crockett."

His eyes drilled into Slocum's. "So I see." He smiled a lazy smile. "You don't care how you spend your time, Marie. Or who with."

His words hit Slocum unpleasantly, startled him. In the Territory cowboys rarely came at him with disrespect; maybe it had to do with the look of him, lean, sinewy, tough, with an aura of danger. This aura sometimes set off a challenge in men driven to find out how good they were. Often they were men searching for glory who felt forced to match themselves against famous gunfighters. Slocum, studying this gunman, wondered if he fitted into this breed, wondered what his game was. His remark

could not go unchallenged, though Slocum had no desire
to challenge it. He didn't care to know him, just hoped
he'd shut up and go away. Slocum had no desire to tangle
with this stranger. It could only delay his pursuit of the
three mangy dogs, could only end up in either bruises
or bloodshed.

Marie guessed as much, for she said, "Say, Crockett,
why don't you tend to your business, and I'll tend to
mine."

Crockett's grin widened. He had read a slow uptake
from Slocum and he liked it. To him it smelled of fear.
He decided to push it. "Don't mind you doin' your business, Marie, but wish you'd show some taste. Don't like
the look of this customer."

The saloon went silent, and men began to edge to the
walls.

Slocum's green eyes glittered. "Mister, I don't know
who you are. But you're talking might careless. Now,
I've got no quarrel with you. I'm feeling good and
wouldn't care to see any unnecessary bleeding round
here. So why don't we forget what's been said, and go
our ways."

Crockett stared at Slocum, a bit unsure. He had figured this man carried a load of fear, but nothing like that
showed in his words. Still, he was disinclined to draw,
and that, to Crockett, had to mean fear.

"You got no quarrel with me, mister, but I got one
with you," the cowboy said.

Slocum's mouth tightened and he stepped away from
Marie, his hands at his side. "What is your quarrel,
sonny?"

Crockett scowled, unnerved by the condescension. He

moved from the bar to face Slocum, feeling rage that he could find no fear in his opponent.

"It's your green hat. I hate a green hat. Can't abide any man who wears one."

Crockett's hand went down like greased lightning to his holster, and he had his gun coming up when he heard the pistol blast, felt the bullet tear his chest. Then he heard nothing, ever again.

Slocum looked at the man on the floor whose chest was pumping out blood. He turned to Marie. "What made him do it? Jealousy?"

She moved close to him. "Crockett was a fast gun in the gang. One of Willie's men."

Slocum walked out of the saloon into the blazing sun, and started up the dusty street toward the hotel. Men were watching him, some smiling. Slocum couldn't help thinking that for men in the Territory, the showdown was their only entertainment, the theater of death. Two gunmen facing each other, ready, because of a moment of rage or a craving for glory, to put their lives on the line.

Slocum didn't care for glory and he didn't draw to prove himself the better man. He'd rather pull back from a pointless showdown; but some men believed that to be fear—in Crockett's case, a fatal mistake. While Slocum tried to avoid a pointless showdown, he couldn't tolerate the bully or the killer.

This Crockett, one of the bunch, had a deluded idea of the speed of his draw. Willie ordered him to kill the man with the green hat, and Crockett was willing; it didn't matter who he was. Crockett was cut from the same vicious stuff as Willie James. With such men you either killed or were killed.

The hotel was a two-story building with peeling brown paint, where a bald-headed clerk with a bulbous nose told him that Miss Keating was in the dining room.

She was about to tackle her dessert, pecan pie and coffee. Slocum sat alongside her and told the waitress to bring him steak, corn, peas, potatoes, biscuits, and after that, a double portion of pie and coffee.

He was startled at the way Diana scowled at him.

Her clear brown eyes looked piercingly at him, and once again he became aware of how good-looking she was. Though her face glowed, she didn't look particularly pleased.

"Seemed to be a long time gone, Slocum," she glowered.

He shrugged. "Takes time to find things out."

"Couldn't take that long to find out they're riding west."

"They could ride south."

She scrutinized him closely, her lips firm. "Did you find out anything?"

His smile was grim. "Yes. You didn't know it, Miss Diana, but you've been harboring a famous gang leader on your ranch."

She scowled. "Is this a joke?"

"No joke. Your Floyd Mercer is really Willie James."

Her eyes widened in shock. She took a full minute before she said, "Willie James! I don't believe that."

"It's true. His brother and cousin were in the bunch. The famous Willie James bunch. Bank robbers."

She looked petrified and it seemed she was running a lot of ideas through her head. "Why the devil did he end up at our ranch, then?" she demanded.

He had thought of that. "The posse of long riders broke that bunch. But some got away. It was said that Willie went underground in Texas, then came up in Arizona. At your ranch. Probably figured he'd stay put till the heat died down. But his brother, Joady, couldn't stay sober, as you found out. That's when they broke loose, took your money and your sister with them."

She turned this over in her mind, her face pale. To Slocum it seemed to hit her harder than it ought. Again he wondered why she hated Floyd—that is, Willie James—so much.

"How'd you find out all this?" she demanded.

"Woman at the saloon, name of Marie, recognized him. Knew him in Dodge City."

Her eyes narrowed. "Why'd she tell you something like that? Seems mighty risky."

He shrugged. "I was able to persuade her. A nice gal."

She glowered. "I'll bet she was. You fool around in a saloon while my Belle is in the bloody hands of outlaws. Damnit, let's go." She stood.

The waitress had just brought out the steak and fixings, and Slocum looked at his food. "Need my strength. Gotta eat."

She threw him a hard look. "I'll be waitin' at the livery."

Slocum nodded, then slowly devoured every morsel in front of him. He ordered a second piece of pecan pie. By this time, he figured, it was too late to do anything about the suffering of Belle, if she was suffering.

He sauntered down the street to the livery where she waited, the horses ready. Her lips were tight.

As he swung over the roan, she said, "Johnson told me what happened at the saloon. Someone in the Willie James gang. They must know about you now, Slocum. I'm sorry if I was a touch ornery, but I worry about Belle."

"I do, too," he said. They picked up the tracks going west, and put the horses into a fast trot.

A hard sun burned down as they rode through arid land where only dry brush and spiky cactus seemed able to thrive. Bulky bronze crags shouldered their way west. In land such as this they had to be careful of water, and twice Slocum stopped to let the horses drink from water poured into his hat from the canteens.

Keystone, which Slocum judged might be the next stop for Willie James, could be half a day off. They were near the trail which the stagecoach took to Keystone. The coach made its stop at Copper Creek, only half an hour away, usually to water the horses. Slocum, who knew the lurking dangers of the land, stopped near a pileup of rocks and climbed to get a long look.

Slocum's piercing gaze swept the rocky, uneven land. In the distance, to the east, he spotted the stagecoach through the shimmering heat. It seemed to be hung there in the sweltering air. He stared hard, then turned his head, searching the land. Nothing moved. A big bird came over with slow, soaring wings, hung over the stage-coach, and began to circle it.

Slocum came down off the rocks. She looked at his face. "What is it?"

"The stagecoach. Not moving. Only thing moving is the buzzard over it."

Her brown eyes looked at him patiently. "Apaches hit the coach?"

"Maybe. Looks like a crisscross, the coach and the Willie James bunch, coming together at the wrong time."

They started to ride.

"Why would Floyd—Willie hit the stagecoach?"

"Why not? He's made a career of that. Just couldn't resist the temptation. Maybe."

"And maybe it wasn't Willie after all, but Apaches."

He smiled. "You don't want Willie to be all that bad, do you?"

Her pretty jaw firmed. "He's no angel, I know. But I don't figger him one for shooting up a stagecoach."

He tried not to smile. She seemed to have a concealed yen for Willie under her hate.

"How rotten do you figure Willie James to be?" he asked.

"Rotten—so you couldn't trust him. Like stealin' and deceivin'."

He shrugged. She had a lot to learn about Willie James. And she might learn some of it when they reached the wagon.

He moved up the pace, figuring whatever else they might find at the coach, they'd at least find barrels of water.

The sun blistered them for another hour before they reached the wagon. By that time four sharp-beaked birds had hit the ground and were reconnoitering.

Slocum wouldn't risk the noise of a bullet. He waved his hands vigorously. They took off, heavy-assed birds who hated to leave the scent of dinner.

Slocum moved close. There were four dead men: the driver, his shotgun rider, and two passengers. The driver had a bloody chest, the shotgun rider a blasted head, and the two passengers, in well-cut suits, were sprawled on their faces. Pockets were turned out and suitcases ransacked.

Diana gazed at the wreckage, her face pale.

"Why'd they do it?"

"They needed water bad. They had four horses and four people. Figured these Eastern dudes might be good pickings, too."

"And I figured Floyd, I mean Willie, for a polecat, but he's much worse."

The water barrel behind the coach had two bulletholes. Nice Willie. He knew he was being trailed, so after the bunch drank and filled their own canteens, he blasted the barrel. No point, he reasoned, to nourish the enemy.

Diana looked at the ugly birds, circling, waiting for a meal.

"We better get them underground."

Slocum gritted his teeth. He was kept busy digging graves for lots of strangers. He pulled his shovel. "I feel sorry for those hungry buzzards. Just hope I get in the position where I can feed them Willie."

After they got the men buried, Slocum closely studied the tracks. "They're just a couple hours ahead of us. Reckon we could close in on them by evening, if we ride hard."

Diana, her face tight, nodded. "I fear for Belle."

# 3

Belle Keating raised the coffee to her lips, glanced at the sun, now low in the sky, then looked at Joady, at his dark, lean face, his brown-yellow eyes that always seemed to glitter with menace, and his hard, lean body, and she felt her heart skip a beat.

The first time she had seen Joady at the ranch, she had felt his magnetism, something she couldn't control. Oh, yes, she was barely sixteen, and Diana often said, wild as a filly in heat, but surely that by itself couldn't explain why he hit her heart like a mule's kick. Oh, it was physical, she had to admit that. He looked at her with his brooding eyes and her knees turned to water.

At the beginning, when he came onto the ranch, brought in by Floyd, who turned out to be Willie, Joady behaved quiet and careful. But she could sense that he was a man with stormy passions. She read it in the fire of his eye, the tautness of his mouth when he looked at her.

She was a bit afraid of him then, and felt it would be most unwise for her to notice him, to josh with him, especially when he said, "There's the most spirited filly on the range."

But she liked him to notice her. The plain fact was most men had begun to notice her; her breasts had pushed out something fierce, her hips widened, and she was feeling strange, wild impulses.

Even Diana had looked at her one day and said, "Good gracious, Belle, you're bustin' out all over." She grinned, then added, "The sap is runnin' strong in you, honey. We're goin' to have to find you a beau real soon."

"I like the look of Joady," she told Diana.

Diana had scowled. "No. Not him. He's not right."

"Why? He's a man. Got red blood in his veins."

Diana shook her head. "Honey, you still got baby fat. This Joady looks like he has a load of dynamite inside him. Not for you."

But as much as Belle adored her sister and respected her advice, when it came to matters of the heart, why, she'd just follow it. Now she had to confess her instinct had put her into a terrible mess. She had flirted with Joady, couldn't help herself. He'd bite his lip, look at her, then Floyd would say something, and Joady would scowl and turn off. Seemed like the one man he feared was Floyd—both loved and feared him.

The night Ketchum brought in the whiskey everything blew up. She remembered it as if it had just happened.

A big yellow moon was hanging out of the sky like

a giant lantern, and the flowers were shooting out perfume.

She could hear the laughing and joshing at the bunkhouse. Their voices drifted on the soft breeze.

So she went out, wearing one of Diana's low-cut dresses that showed her shoulders and plenty of her hefty breasts. And, as luck would have it, Joady came out, headed for his bunk when he spotted her. He was drunk as a coot, no denying that, because he staggered. But at sight of her, he stopped in his tracks and stared. And she stared back, bold as a hussy; she didn't know why, but her blood was singing and her body was yearning. She didn't know what devil goaded her. But Joady seemed to know, because he came toward her quiet as a snake, his dangerous brown eyes glowing with the fire that always fascinated her. Then he reached her. His voice was low, thrilling.

"Miss Belle, you ain't got a right to make a man feel this way."

"What d'ye mean by that, Joady?" she said softly.

He came close, and his manly smell was strong; it put a spell on her.

"I'll show you what I mean, little lady." And he put his strong arms around her, pressed against her. She felt him through his Levi's, sturdy and powerful, and if she had any will, it just went right out of her. She was ready to do anything he wanted. He kissed her, and she felt herself melting. "Come with me, pretty Belle," he whispered in her ear, and led her to his bunk, locked the door. And she knew what was happening, even wanted it. She couldn't help it, it was her yearning. And he knew she wanted it. He hiked her dress up, pulled her drawers down, and he was big, brutal almost, but still it was the most exciting thing that had ever happened in her young life. Did she blame him? Not at all. She'd just been pushed hard by nature, for better or worse.

The trouble started when Floyd came in. He swung at Joady, knocked him down.

"You spoiled everything, you and this hot-blooded kid. Now we gotta go. Get Ketch, the horses, and I'll go up to the big house and see what I can do."

Before they started to ride, Joady said, "You're comin' with us, Belle."

She said, "No, I couldn't do a thing like that. But you ought to stay. I'll try to fix it with Diana."

He laughed. "You loco? She'd try to skin me alive. And I wouldn't care much for that. Might make me mean."

"Well," Belle said, "I'm not sure I can go. Diana would whale the tar outa me."

"Not while you're with me, honeybelle," he said. "I'll take good care of yuh. Very good." And his eyes glittered.

She was in a knot about it, not knowing what to do, a bit fearful of Joady, who could be brutal. But she just ached to have his arms around her, just ached for it. And that was what he did, telling her she was coming even if he had to drag her.

So she figured she'd go and see what would come of it.

But she figured without Floyd who, when he came back with Ketchum stared at her, then said to Joady, "What the hell d'ya think you're doin'?"

"She's comin'," Joady said.

Floyd didn't get excited; his eyes just looked flat. "Are you loco? She'd hang 'round our necks like a roped steer. We gotta travel fast and light."

Joady's jaw went hard. "Don't care about nothin'. She's comin'."

Floyd bit his lip, seeing the iron in Joady. "You sawed-off little polecat. There's a dozen fillies out there for that hot dick of yours. Why this one? She ain't fully growed yet."

Joady's tone was flat. "She's the one, Willie. She goes."

Belle didn't know till later why Joady called him Willie, but Floyd glared at him. "You're one thick-brain, Joady, and I'm gettin' mighty tired tryin' to keep you alive."

"Go your ways, if you want, Willie," Joady said sullenly. "I'm takin' the filly, come hell or high water."

Floyd, or Willie, took a deep breath. "There's no tellin' what'll come after us, Joady. The lady won't sit still for it."

"Didn't know a filly could put fear into Big Willie," Joady sneered.

Belle began to think of Floyd as Willie, and Willie showed his teeth. "You're a mule-brained kid, and I'm cursed havin' you as a brother. Musta been the devil wished you on me. Take her and be damned. Give her the bay. And you're responsible for keepin' her movin'. Anyone follow us, she gets tied until we clear it."

And that's what happened; she didn't really know till later, from what they said and what they did that she was in the hands of Willie James, his brother, and their cousin.

The famous outlaw Willie James. And they tried to hang her cousin Jake, who'd come after them with Diana. If only she'd known. They were cool desperadoes—she'd watched them, just hours ago, shoot down the men in the stagecoach like you'd potshoot rabbits. And then Joady growled at her, "We needed the water. Did you want to die of thirst, missy?"

The truth was, she'd come away with terrible men. And she feared what might happen. Yet she still felt the fascination of Joady. Still thrilled at his touch, craved his embrace. It was crazy. She was crazy, but that's how she was.

"Are you goin' to sit there dreamin', Belle?" Joady growled. "Take some jerky. By tomorrow we'll be in Keystone and eat some decent grub."

Willie looked at her with his gray steely eyes and shook his head. "Joady, you ain't yet learned how to get a hold on your lust. And you better learn it."

Joady's eyes were heavy-lidded. "Why?"

Willie glared, "'Cause one day, your cock is gonna cook your goose, that's why."

"Won't ever happen, Willie." Joady patted his holster. "Don't know what you're feared of. Just one lucky cowboy and the lady."

Willie nodded. "That cowboy pulls a fast gun, 'cause Crockett's gone. And Diana can shoot the eyes outa a snake at fifty yards. Never underestimate the other guy. Always tole you that, Joady."

"Okay, Willie. We won't do that," Joady said, and stood up and stretched.

The rifle shot echoed off the crags around them, and the bullet hit Joady's left shoulder, nipped two inches of flesh. It flung him over the fire, but he rolled off; his vest and shirt got singed and blackened by the ash.

Diana's fears about Belle made them push hard, eating on the run, and they made such good headway that by sundown Slocum sighted the smoke of a campfire.

The land was pockmarked with boulders and dry brush. A serrated ridge went high against the mountains, with sites for a long look.

Taking his rifle, Slocum swung off the roan and climbed the ridge to a jutting rock. Diana picketed the horses, then also decided to come up with her rifle. She climbed, sure-footed as an Indian.

They stared toward the campsite. Willie had cleverly picked an incline sheltered by stone and brush. All Slocum could see, a good distance off, was the tops of three hats. He looked at clouds scudding across the sky driven by a southwester and at the sun sinking to the towering peaks of the Catalinas. It wouldn't be long before good shooting light would be gone.

He looked at Diana holding her rifle, staring with clear brown eyes at the campfire. She was the deadeye, he remembered, splitting the hangman's noose from around his neck.

"Wouldn't surprise me, Diana, if you could shoot the tail off a polecat a mile away." He pointed to the campfire. "Okay, deadeye, let's see you shoot."

She studied the campsite. "Nothin' to shoot at, Slocum."

"They're sittin', that's why. Sooner or later, someone will stand. Get that deadeye of yours ready."

Her jaw clenched; she didn't seem to like it.

He said, "Best to cut down the size of the other side quick as we can, Miss Diana."

She thought about it. "If I miss, they'll know we're just in back of them."

"Where else do they think we are?"

Her eyes fluttered. She wasn't happy about it, and he wondered why. She raised her rifle and sighted, just for practice. Then, as if on cue, someone who looked like Joady stood up and stretched. She held her breath, but didn't squeeze the trigger.

"Shoot!" he said.

She squeezed the trigger.

Seconds ticked off. Nothing happened. Then the sound of the shot rattled off the crags, but Joady kept stretching. Then he grabbed at his shoulder and plunged forward.

Everyone at the campsite ducked out of sight.

Slocum stared at her.

Her mouth was crunched.

She had missed—the deadeye. Slocum found it hard to believe. It was a long shot, yes; but he would have bet his last dime that her bullet would go true.

Why?

The clouds were scuttling over their heads, and the sun started to hit the peaks. In just a few minutes, shooting light wouldn't be good. There was nothing to shoot at anyway.

The James bunch stayed down, out of sight, waiting for the dark. They had rotten position, didn't know where the bullet came from; there was nothing for them to do until dark.

Slocum hunched down behind the outcropping rocks

and lit a havana. He smoked calmly.

Her face scrunched up as if she had swallowed something bitter.

"What's eatin' you, Slocum?"

He shook his head slowly. "Can't understand how a deadeye can split a rope but can't hit a target big as a man."

"I didn't miss."

"You didn't?"

She shrugged. "It happens sometimes."

"Only because the deadeye *wants* to miss."

She flushed. "Are you saying I missed Joady because I *wanted* to?"

"You sure hated to pull that trigger." He looked at the sun now backlighting the peaks, touching them with yellow fire. "That was Joady," he said. "The man who started your troubles with Belle. The man who put a noose around my neck."

She grimaced. "Next time *you* do it."

He smiled. It was pointless to make a fuss. It would spoil the hunting. "It's all right, Diana. You did get a hunk of him; looked like the left shoulder. If he's hurt, he won't be useful to Willie for a time." But he was thinking that as long as Joady's right trigger finger worked, he'd be dangerous.

The sky flamed briefly, then all color drained out.

After sunset night hit the land almost with a crunch. They climbed off the ridge in dim moonlight. Slocum, with his instinct for caution, moved camp to the left of the shooting site in case, during the night, Willie might reconnoiter.

He slept that night with part of his mind listening, and could hear the howl of the coyotes and the scream of the nighthawk.

Early daylight, he climbed the ridge. The campsite was clear.

Diana had coffee on the fire when he came back. They drank in silence, and the sky began to flame orange as the sun came up.

"Gonna be another hot one," he said.

She sipped her coffee.

He rubbed the roan's haunches, waiting for her to talk.

"I had Joady in my sights," she said finally, "but couldn't shoot. Want to know why?" Her voice was soft.

He looked at her.

"Because I didn't want to shoot Joady from way off. No satisfaction in that. I want to *see* him when he's hit. Close up."

He had to smile. It explained things better. She'd rather miss than hit Joady from long range. So it wasn't a streak of softness. She had a hard grudge, like him. Still, he was thinking, shooting was a man's business. He'd made a mistake asking her to do it. He should have done it, put Joady out. Now they knew they were tailed tight, and would be wary, maybe try an ambush of their own.

Things had got more complicated.

When they started to ride, the sky looked steel-bright, without clouds. They picked up Willie's tracks, easy to follow, and moved briskly. In time, the sun started to feel fierce.

Studying the tracks, Slocum figured that Willie didn't

seem interested in tangling with them just yet. He seemed to have something else in mind.

By noon the sun was broiling the earth and living creatures of the land began to crawl underground or into shade. Sweat glistened on the flanks of the horses and Slocum slowed the pace. He took time to search for water and found a slow, trickling stream. They filled the canteens, gave water to the horses from their hats.

"How far to Keystone?" she asked.

"Hope we make it by sundown. But moving in this heat won't be easy."

He scanned the land: trees and grass nearby, parched plain to the front, and high ground with serrated rocks on the sides.

The roan's ears went up, and Slocum felt a surge of uneasiness. Instinct made him turn quickly; then he heard the swish of the arrow, felt the pain in his left arm. His right hand flashed to his holster and he fired at the glimpse of the Apache who had slipped behind a cover of rock, on the high ground.

They scrambled behind a big black rock.

"You're hit," she said.

The arrow stuck out of his flesh near his elbow. He broke the stem, drew his knife, cut into his arm, and pulled out the arrowhead. He tied his neckerchief like a tourniquet to stop the blood flow.

Then he cursed. He had seen the roan's ears go up and it should have told him something. There had been tracks at the spring, but he concentrated on the water. He was getting careless, and you didn't surive that.

Diana was looking unhappy.

"A scratch," he said. "Guess the other Apache never

did go back to his tribe. Found the grave of his comrade, and came after us, looking for revenge. Revenge comes first with the Apache." He shook his head.

"What now?"

He examined the ascending rocks. "Have to go after him."

Her eyes clouded; she didn't like it. "He knows that we know he's there. He might just go away."

"But he won't. It's the way they are. They stick to the end."

Her head turned. "What about Willie? He might get away."

"Not as long as I can track." Slocum's voice was hard. He studied the high ground. "The Apache. I'd better go after him. We'll never know when he'll strike again. That can be bad."

"What do I do?"

"Stick with the horses. Keep your eyes open. If I don't come back when the sun's down, go like hell for Keystone."

She scowled. "Don't like it. And you better come back."

He smiled. "It'll be all right. See you soon."

# 4

His gun ready, Slocum peered at the rise where he'd glimpsed the Apache. Nothing. Just serrated rocks against high ground. What could be behind those rocks—a cave, an Indian trail, a hiding place from where the Apache, wiliest of warriors, could ambush his enemy?

A deadly setup. In the territory, you had to prepare for attack by hostiles, and if you didn't have the craft, your goose was cooked. An Apache might have bow and arrow, and you the gun, but it was not the weapon that won the victory. If you were tracked by an Apache, you were in a chess game. Each move had its counter, and the smart move left your enemy exposed, ready to be destroyed.

This Apache, Slocum felt, was deadly. He had managed to be somewhere else when Slocum shot and buried his comrade. He had discovered the grave, swore ven-

geance, found the trail of the paleface enemy, and followed through pitiless heat. His arrow would have killed
Slocum if the roan's ears hadn't catapulted a warning so
that Slocum twisted his body. Though this Apache didn't
have a gun, he knew a dozen ways to kill.

Slocum moved warily out of his rock shelter to the
rise. He could get there using cover, but he'd be exposed
part of the time. Was the Apache still lurking behind that
outjutting rock? While Slocum had worked to get the
arrow out, the Apache could have gone anywhere. But
Slocum had to reach that jutting rock and, if he wasn't
there, track him. He couldn't fly; he had to leave prints.

Gun ready, Slocum moved lightly from rock to brush.
He'd glimpsed the Apache's face: broad-boned, thick
nose, high cheeks, a band holding the long dark hair. A
muscled warrior. Might be the same one who had killed
Jake Kelly, Diana's kin. This redskin was a survivor,
therefore the most dangerous.

Slocum zigzagged from boulder to brush. He studied
the serrated rocks. Where could a smart Indian wait, his
knife or bow ready? It was a long run to that jutting
boulder, and Slocum realized how wily the Apache had
been to shoot from behind it, in case he missed and a
hunt like this would happen.

Now Slocum sprinted. He was in the open, half expecting an arrow. But it didn't happen. Behind the rock—
no Apache! And he had smoothed his prints.

Slocum stood petrified. Where in hell had he gone?
Apaches moved silently as snakes and struck just as deadly.
Slocum studied the ground and found a faint moccasin
print on a rock. His move was west, not higher, as Slocum expected. He felt a quiver of discomfort; he had no

idea of where this redskin had gone. Did he go west, then go up, or did he retrace his steps? Go down?

*Down!*

Slocum froze. For the first time he looked back over a space of thirty yards, to where he'd left Diana.

Gone.

His skin tingled. His trigger finger tightened.

His first impulse was to race down, but he was dealing with a crafty foe. Where in hell had she gone? Was it possible . . .

Ready to fire at sound or sight, he started down the serrated rocks, his thoughts spurting. And he didn't like them.

When he reached the ground, a string of curses ripped from his lips.

The Apache had Diana. And the horses.

He stood still, teeth clenched, feeling the blood seething in his veins. This Apache, a crafty devil, had outfoxed him, knew his moves before he had made them, and in a clever maneuver, the Apache had put himself in a position to circle Diana. He had figured the paleface, who had not been hit fatally by his arrow, would climb in pursuit. Maybe he would leave the woman behind with the horses. When the paleface did exactly that, the Apache just moved silently behind Diana, sacked her, and made off. All that time Slocum was sneaking up the high ground, being crafty and clever, and finding nothing.

The trick and nerve of it amazed Slocum. He stood there thinking. He looked at the hoofprints. Walking prints. Why not running prints? He was an Apache, had his own mustang pony nearby; he would dump Diana over her horse, go to his pony. What might happen then was something Slocum didn't care to visualize.

Every second counted. His gaze swept the land. Bushes, thickets, boulders—all good for camouflage and deception. The Apache had picked his ground; he'd picked the spring, knowing Slocum couldn't pass that up, and then these thickets for concealment.

Slocum stood still, petrified, thinking.

The Apache could never have raced the horses out. Sound would betray him. He studied the surrounding thickets. Nearby was the big curving rock, hiding the land beyond it.

He stared at this rock, looked at the ridge over it, for a way to climb the south side, which might let him spy the north side. He needed to get high so he could see down, also to get a long view of the land, to spot the Apache, if he was still riding.

Silently as a ghost, he went back twenty yards, circled until he reached the rocks, and climbed, edging south. He had taken a calculated risk, and if he was wrong, it would be a terrible waste of time, considering what might happen to Diana in the hands of this Apache.

He crept softly and silently to the edge of the big curved rock, and never put his foot down until he was sure of the firm stone. No pebbles, no loose grit, no sound. Surprise had to be everything, if he guessed right. If wrong, it would be like shooting without a bullet in his gun.

Now, at the edge, he leaned over, to peer out.

Nothing.

His disappointment was intense, and he cursed silently. But something fluttered at the edge of his mind, and he looked at the outcropping rock that blocked part of his vision. His nerves tightened. It seemed like the soft whisper of a sound floated up. To see, he would have to edge over six more feet. He started to creep slowly, two inches at a time.

Then he saw them.

Diana was on the ground, unconscious, her Levi's pulled down, her shirt open, exposing her breasts.

The Apache had her gun in his hand, and was waiting at the edge of the curve of the crag, waiting for Slocum's inevitable appearance, ready to blow his head off.

Then the Apache, because he was a man, couldn't help glancing back down at the naked paleface woman, at her physical beauty.

Slocum stared at him, gun in hand, waiting.

And, just as Slocum had expected, the Apache's sixth sense made him look up. His brown eyes glared for one hypnotic moment into the green eyes looking down at him. The brown eyes widened with shock, and with amazing speed, he brought the gun up to fire. But Slocum's gun was already pointing and his bullet was on its way, burying itself in the center of his forehead, crashing into the brain. He quivered like a tree struck by lightning, then he fell like one, dead before he hit the ground.

At Keystone, they walked to a table in the rowdy saloon, and a lot of eyes turned to look at the three big men in black hats, and the delicate young filly. The men were smart enough to say nothing, though it puzzled them plenty to see such a sight. The aura of menace about the three men kept the drinkers discreetly quiet. Recognition of Willie James did it, too.

The bartender brought two bottles and glasses to the table. "Nice to see you, Willie," he said in a soft voice.

Willie James nodded. "You, too, Sam. Been expecting Biggers and Snouts. Seen them?"

"Not a sign of them yet, Willie."

Willie James grunted and his cold gray eyes stared at the drinkers at the bar. The men who recognized him turned quickly, but the others looked curiously at men who would calmly bring a sweet-looking young filly like Belle into the rowdy saloon. She was so unlike the painted hussies sitting there that some of the cowboys had to stare at her fresh pink face and wonder.

One black-haired cowboy with dark eyes, wearing a brown leather vest, kept staring at Belle, then at the men, and grinding his teeth.

He muttered under his breath, poured whiskey into his glass, and gulped it. Then he turned to his neighbor and said in a low voice, "I hate to see a thing like that. A girl like her with those mean-looking hombres."

"Stay out of it, Charlie," the other cowboy said.

"She reminds me of my kid sister, Daisy," Charlie said. "Imagine her fallin' into the hands of skunks like them? Doesn't it make you sick, Smitty?"

"You got a sister like that, Charlie? Sure'd like to meet up with her."

Charlie threw him a vicious look.

"No offense, Charlie," Smitty said quickly. "But if I were you, I wouldn't mess with them."

Charlie had a small black mustache, black hair, a powerful chest, and muscular arms. He studied the men at the table. "Why not?"

"Tell you why not," said Smitty. "That man in the

short black hat with the scarred face is none other than
Willie James."

Charlie's eyes narrowed. "The bank robber? That him?"

"Yeah, and if I were you, I wouldn't even think about
him. He'd pick you off in the flick of a lamb's tail."

Charlie had had too much whiskey to believe that.
He'd always been fast with a gun, had never met anyone
faster. At this moment he was feeling ferocious. That
was how the booze sometimes hit him. And, staring at
the girl, he kept thinking that men like these could grab
Daisy, his own sister, and she'd be with them, just like
that poor girl, who, he sensed, looked nervy. They had
probably grabbed her, dragged her along, and now she
was done for. Why should a man like Willie James run
things the way he wanted? He didn't look that fast, and
it'd sure be a service to the Territory to clean out a killer
like Willie.

Suddenly he was on his feet, moving slowly and carefully toward the corner table. Until that moment the table
had been surrounded by space, as if nobody dared break
into the charmed circle.

The cowboy suddenly moving toward the table grabbed
everyone's attention, and the noise of the saloon seemed
to turn off like a light.

The men at the table looked at the black-haired cowboy with eyes cold and curious.

Charlie stopped in front of Willie, who stared at him,
at his gun and his hands down at his sides.

"What's on your mind, mister?" Joady said.

Charlie ignored him, his eyes on Willie. "Don't you
feel any shame bringing this young girl into the saloon?"
he asked.

A slow smile twisted Willie's features. "No, I don't, mister."

Charlie's face was grim. "Guess you don't feel shame at anything, a man like you. You're Willie James, ain't you?"

Joady rose to his feet.

"Sit down," Willie said.

Joady glowered, then sat down.

Willie's gray eyes fastened on Charlie. "You're a young fella who's had too much whiskey, and your head ain't clear. Don't think about things that ain't your business. Why don't you go back to your whiskey, jest so you can live a little longer."

"And," said Charlie, "I'm thinking a man like you who's been robbin' and killin' and mebbe stealing a young girl like that has lived too long already. Time to put an end to the likes of Willie James. Stand up."

Willie looked at him, then his eyes slipped to the men at the door, and a smile twisted his lips.

"If I stand up you're dead, mister," Willie said.

Charlie's jaw clenched, his hands poised at his holster. "Stand up and be damned," he said.

Then a curious thing happened. Willie James stood up, but did not draw. That didn't stop Charlie, whose hand streaked for his holster; he had every excuse to pull his gun, but even as he brought it out two pistols roared and Charlie was whipsawed like a rag doll, one side to the other, then pitched face down on the floor of the saloon, dead.

Willie, who still hadn't drawn his gun, glanced at the two men with their smoking guns; he'd seen them come into the saloon and mingle with the crowd when Charlie confronted him at the table.

All innocence, Willie looked at the dead cowboy, then at the two men, their guns still out.

"Why'd you do that, Biggers?" Willie asked.

"Couldn't let that polecat shoot a man who didn't draw, Willie," Biggers said, grinning.

"You took a helluva chance, boss," said Snouts, the other man, "not pulling your gun."

Willie's face was cool. "Put my life on the line. That's what I do for my men. And what I expect from them." He sat down calmly, and the two men, with a careful look at the drinkers, also sat at the table.

They lugged dead Charlie out the back door, and within minutes the chatter of the saloon was back to usual.

Joady picked up his glass and said, "Willie, I'm jest expressin' my honest opinion. You're a danged fool for not pullin' your gun at a time like that."

Willie smiled and his cheekbones, scarred from fist-fights in saloons, creased to give him a sinister look. "That's the difference between us, Joady. I take the chance, but only when I figger it's the right one."

Joady shook his head. "Shoulda let me blast that pole-cat when he came over."

Willie leaned forward. "What if he was a faster gun, Joady? He had to be fast, since he gambled on takin' me on. No slow gun is gonna do that, is he, Joady? The way I did, he never got a chance to show how fast he was, did he?"

Joady stared at his brother with a curious expression which brought Willie back suddenly to a night on their father's farm in Missouri. Willie James had piercing gray eyes that looked like they knew the evil in men's hearts and figured there was nothing else.

He and his brother, Joady, were raised in Missouri by an iron-fisted father, Luther James. The father never forgave Joady who, to get born, destroyed his mother. Luther dulled his pain with liquor and worked out his drunken rages by whipping the boys for any reason.

The night that came back to Willie's memory as he sat in the saloon was when the father told fourteen-year-old Joady to bring him another jug of liquor. The jug, by evil chance, slipped from his young fingers and smashed on the rocks. In a drunken rage, the father began to beat Joady almost senseless. Willie watched with his cold gray eyes for a while, then picked up a nearby hammer and drove it three inches into his father's skull.

Joady stared with fear and love at his brother. "What are we gonna do now, Willie?"

Willie stood silent, staring at his dead father sprawled on the ground, his coarse face still distorted with rage.

"Jest killed a drunken hyena, Joady. Think of it like that. We'll bury him, and then we'll ride to Kansas."

That night they left, rode toward Wichita, living off the land, doing odd jobs, hating it. Mostly they loafed, pretended to be older, hung out with drifters, wandered down into the Territories, learning how to survive.

Willie learned, too, after a time, that an ounce of thought was worth a pound of fighting. Using his head, he started to collect desperate men, good with guns.

Now, sitting at the table, Willie let his mind run back over the good days, bank robbing, train robbing, doing it the smart way, keeping down the killings. He had made the Willie James gang such a nuisance that the government organized the posse of long riders, and that was how they broke the gang, hanging some, jailing some. But they never caught Willie, brother Joady, or cousin Ketchum. These three drifted into the Arizona Territory where one day Willie, while watching a bank, saw Diana Keating. She was a comely filly with clean brown eyes, a saucy mouth, and a hefty bosom. He learned her name, that she owned the big Keating ranch west of town, the Bar M.

Willie did some thinking, figured it would be smart to hide out on her ranch till the heat on the James gang cooled down. Maybe he could score points with the pretty missy.

So he arranged, after Diana Keating came out of Levy's Merchandise store and mounted up, for Joady to start a commotion, which made Diana's horse streak crazily up Main Street. And who would be riding by but this gray-eyed, good-looking man of steel, who grabbed her wild horse and gentled him.

Grateful Diana quickly discovered that the stranger, who called himself Floyd Mercer, was looking for work. Her father, recently dead, had left her in dire need of a good man, and she offered him a job. He soon brought in Joady and Ketchum.

It was a fine place to go underground until the posse's search for the Willie James bunch petered out.

By that time, Diana had become dependent on Willie, willing to share with him her heart and her land.

Willie James gritted his teeth and lifted his glass of whiskey. The loud sounds of the saloon filtered into his mind, to blur his memories. Still, he couldn't help thinking about Joady, always a hardcase, who, in spite of warnings, couldn't keep away from the young filly, Belle. Joady kicked everything to pieces the night he got drunk and taught young Belle the pleasures of sin.

Willie sighed. He loved his brother but the lad was a mulebrain and sometimes a curse.

Willie looked at Biggers, a hawk-nosed, rawboned cowboy with pale gray eyes that stared at the world as if he didn't know what it meant. He sat at the table, pouring himself a whiskey. "Gotta hand it to you, Willie, you got nerve."

Willie nodded, thinking it did take nerve to run a gang of gunmen. Such men were hard heads, firebrands, always ready to flare up, given any reason. To make a bunch work, you needed discipline, and there had to be one man in control—one man, one mind, one will. That was how he'd built the Willie James bunch.

As for Biggers, he had picked him up in Dodge City, a good gun, a gutsy fighter. Willie always sifted men for the gang; he wanted men with guts, no crazies.

"What about Burt, Mike, and Tom?" Willie asked. "You were s'posed to meet at Arrowhead, then come here."

"They didn't show," Biggers said. "We gave 'em five hours. Left word to meet at Tucson."

Willie lit a cigarillo. The bunch had been mangled; not many were left. Well, he could do plenty with seven good men. It took less than that to rob a bank. And he was thinking hard about the bank at Tucson. But first things first. There was the sticking mangy dog, Slocum, on their trail, and the plain fact was you couldn't work anything until he was wiped out. Slocum must have knocked off Crockett, so he was no slouch when it came to pulling a gun. And Diana was a deadly shot. But she could be managed, once that polecat Slocum was out of the way. Slocum had to go down before they could feel safe.

Snouts was looking at Belle, and Joady didn't like it. Snouts was a red-faced, big-nosed cowboy with a hard, powerful body. He wore black boots and his gun had a polished handle. He started to grin, looking at Belle, and Joady bristled.

"Don't say anything, Snouts."

Snout's eyes widened innocently. "Not thinkin' a thing."

"That's Belle, Joady's filly," said Willie. He stroked his chin. "Belle, you go up to the general store and pick up some extra jerky. We'll be along soon."

"S'pose I didn't want to go, Willie," she said.

Willie smiled. She had an edge of toughness that he admired. "Do us a favor, Belle. We'd 'preciate it a lot."

Joady stood up. "I'll go with you, Belle."

Willie frowned. "Jes' to the door, Joady. We need you here."

Willie watched them move for a moment, then said, "I got in mind a bank job at Tucson. But we got a pesky coyote stickin' to our tracks, and we gotta shake him. We need a quick gun to do it, Biggers."

"Who is the man?" asked Biggers.

"Man called Slocum."

Biggers frowned. "John Slocum? A Georgia man?"

Willie looked at him. "You know him?"

"Slocum. Yeah, I know of him." Biggers said.

Willie's eyes narrowed.

Biggers grimaced. "Not an easy man to knock over. He rode with Quantrill. Did you know that? A hot gun, they say."

Willie's jaw tightened. "A Reb. I figured there was iron in him."

Joady had come back to the table and was listening.

Biggers nodded. "He fought with the Georgia Regulars. A sharpshooter. They used him to pick off the bluecoat officers."

Joady lifted his glass. "He didn't look that tough to me. Remember how easy we nailed him, Willie? Got a rope on his neck before he knew what hit him."

Willie scowled. "That's 'cause he respected the badge of the marshal. Won't work again. I thought him a nervy coyote, the way he said, 'You're a marshal like I'm a horse thief.' Too bad we didn't know who he was. We figured him to be Jake Kelly." He looked at Ketchum. "You went back to scout. What'd you find?"

Ketchum said, "Kelly got hit by Apaches in the Squaw country. I saw the tracks and the grave. Figger that Slocum buried him. Musta picked up his green hat, after."

Willie grunted. "Well, Slocum sticks to us like a hungry coyote. We gotta get rid of him."

There was a long silence while the men lifted their glasses to drink. Ketchum stared at Joady. "You're always shootin' from the hip, Joady. Don't know what you're doin'. I tole you, the time you wanted to rush into hanging, to make sure."

"Make sure of what, Ketch?"

"Make sure we had the right man. The way he talked, I figgered we might be makin' a mistake."

Joady glared. "You're always needlin' me, Ketch."

"Jes' askin' you not to run before you think," Ketch said, lifting his glass. "Like the dumb way you pulled Belle outa the ranch. The wrong move, jest like Willie tole you. But you're a mulehead."

Joady's dark eyes glittered. "Ketch, I let you say things I'd let no other man. It's cause you're my kin. But there's a limit to what I'll take. Keep that in mind."

Ketch glowered. "I, too, keep thinkin' you're my blood, otherwise some of your crazy ways wouldn't go down easy with me."

Willie watched, stroking his chin.

Joady's mouth was tight. "It's not me, Ketch, that's botherin' you. It's Belle. I seen the way you look at her. I see what's in your eyes. You're jealous."

"Yeah, I'm jealous—but not the way you're thinkin'. 'Cause you got a beautiful young girl there, and you're treatin' her like a squaw."

"Damn your eyes, Ketch, I'm warnin' you."

Willie slapped his hand on the table. "Listen, you two locos, I don't want any of this feudin'. It's feudin' that breaks up a bunch. We got power when we act together for the good of the bunch. But the moment we start feudin', it's the beginin' of the end. We're still the Willie James bunch, with a rep all over the Territory. But we start fightin' among ourselves, we're done for.

"Now we got a coyote on our tail, this Slocum. And he ain't gonna fade away. We gotta nail him. One gun won't be enough, Snouts. You and Biggers will hafta take him down, 'cause he don't know either of you. Set him up. You know how, like we did with Bloody Bill in Fort Worth. Slocum's a stranger, he comes into this saloon, askin' for Willie James. He'll do that; he's got nerve. You both be ready." Willie raised his glass and drank, wiped his mouth with his sleeve.

"I'm trying to think about how to knock off the bank in Tucson, but it's hard to think clear with a hungry coyote trackin' you hard. The way you shoot him down won't matter a fig to the polecats in this town. He's a stranger who jest got too uppity. You know how to do it, boys. You've done it before." He stood up, gave the sign to his bunch. "We'll meet at the fork near Red River, then go on to Tucson." He grinned. "It's got a beautiful bank."

Slocum looked at Diana on the ground, her face pale, eyes closed, breathing quietly. A red bruise flared on her right forehead, where the Apache hit her, knocking her cold. From the way he had stripped Diana, that redskin had more than vengeance in mind. The Apache had lost three comrades to the paleface, and he had some nasty ideas about how to pay him back. He'd been clever, this Apache, and it was easy to imagine what might have happened if he got in the first bullet. Slocum could see himself being forced to watch sinister doings.

Diana stirred

Slocum stared at her. Her shirt had been ripped back, showing her breasts, beautiful white mounds, topped with pink nipples. Her Levi's were pulled down, showing finely moulded thighs, the pink lips between them scarcely covered by short, curly brown hair.

Slocum felt a tingling in his Levi's and gritted his teeth. They were on a trail of revenge, hunting a crafty gang leader and his men. It would be hard to think of a more dangerous mission. He'd be a dumb lummox to let lust muddle his thinking. If you think about a roll in the hay, you end up pushing daisies, he told himself. Anyway, Diana had done nothing to give him reason to start lusting. He never saw a woman so hard to get some iron into Willie James. Couldn't just be the money he stole, or even grabbing Belle, her sister. Maybe Willie had done Diana wrong, and hell hath no fury like a woman scorned, as the saying goes.

The horses were picketed in a nearby thicket, and Slocum pulled whiskey from his saddlebag. Some color had returned to Diana's cheeks by now. He lifted her head and put the whiskey cup carefully to her lips. Her eyes fluttered and she looked groggy. He gazed at her body, then bit his lip. He gave her another sip and her eyes opened. She looked dazed, then smiled. Then suddenly she became aware of her nudity, sat up, startled, bringing her arms to cover herself. When she saw the dead Apache, she let out a small cry. Quickly, she buttoned her shirt, pulled up her Levi's. Then she winced as her hand went to the bruise on her head.

She looked at the Apache again. "He hit me from behind. I never heard him. A light just went out in my head, Slocum. But you saved me. Thank you, Slocum. God, what did he have in mind!"

Slocum smiled. She'd saved his life when she split that hanging rope. He didn't feel as if he had yet paid off that debt.

"I'm feared that Apache had a few nasty ideas in mind. He didn't trail us all this time just for the pleasure. He lost three comrades, and was gonna make the palefaces pay. He was one smart Indian, but he made a bad mistake."

Diana, by now modestly covered, looked at him. "What mistake?"

"The mistake most men make—a woman."

Her brow furrowed and her voice took on a slight chill. "What mistake?"

"The fatal mistake. A woman makes a man lose his concentration when he needs it most."

Her lips twisted. "What do you mean?"

"That Apache wanted to destroy the white man hunting him, but he couldn't keep his mind on the job one hundred percent. His mind kept going back to you, a beautiful, sexy white woman, at his mercy. It's why I got close enough to get him before he got me."

She thought about it. "I muddled his head a bit, is that what you mean, Slocum?"

He grinned. "Lying there, the way you did, distracted him, gave me the edge. And the only way to stay alive in the Territory, I have discovered, is, when you're in a showdown, to try and get an edge."

"I don't s'pose a man like you would be distracted by an unclothed woman." Her voice was silky. "But I'm glad to have you as a partner, Slocum. You're smart and you're fast, and I reckon that's what we need to get Willie James."

Slocum stroked his chin. "Trouble is, Willie's smart and fast, too. He didn't get to be the boss of the James bunch by being slow and dumb. We got to figure he's gonna be a bag of tricks."

She nodded. "Yes, he's tricky. A tricky devil." Her voice was hard.

Again he was tempted to dig and find out what was

eating her about Willie James, but something put him off.

Then he noticed the buzzard flying overhead, its wings spread, begin a slow circular soar. He sighed. "Better be burying this brave real good. Getting tired of avenging Apaches."

He put the body over the roan, found a suitable crevice, dug a deep grave, dropped the body, smoothed the ground, and threw small stones over it. The camouflage looked good, but how would it look to the eagle eye of an Apache? He'd just have to hope a wandering redskin didn't discover the grave to start more vengeance.

They picked up Willie's tracks, headed for Keystone, and rode at an even pace. The sun was on a downward spiral, and the canyons in the distance, gilded by light, looked like cathedrals. As they came nearer to Keystone, the sun slipped lower, and the sky became flaming smears of orange, primrose, and purple.

The silence was intense in this awesome theater of Nature.

Then Diana said, "Did you call me a beautiful woman, Slocum? I think I heard you say that. Did you mean it, or is that the bull you use talkin' to the ladies?"

He had to smile. "I always speak my mind, Miss Diana."

"Always?"

He nodded.

She gave him a broad smile and they started into Keystone.

# 5

Slocum pushed open the batwing doors of Sam O'Leary's saloon and walked in. It was Friday and cowboys and wranglers had come in from nearby ranches and after a day of hustling cows and horses were ready to relax. They did it with drinking, bragging, fighting, playing cards, and playing with wicked ladies.

The bartender came over to Slocum and peered at him sharply. "Sam O'Leary. What's your pleasure, mister?"

"Whiskey."

Sam put a bottle and glass on the bar. "Jest hit town, I reckon."

Slocum nodded, lifted his glass, let his eyes go slowly over the men at the bar, the men playing cards. Neither Willie nor his men were here. He was looking not only for Willie's men but for something else. What he'd seen, for example, in the bartender's eyes: more than just idle curiosity. He tossed off his drink and his glance again went casually back to the cardplayers. One of them, a hawk-nosed, rawboned cowboy, facing the bar, had sneaked a second look.

Slocum knew that when he walked into a saloon like this anything could happen. He acted lazy, relaxed, but his nerves were taut, his eyes alert.

That hawk-nosed cowboy had the kind of look Slocum often found in gunmen. In his mind, they were a breed apart; men who lived by the gun had a deep reckless vein. This cowboy had it.

Slocum filled his glass.

Sam, the bartender, smiled, mopped the wood in front of him. "Riding through, mister?"

"Could be."

Sam's smile faded. He had a lot of experience working the saloon, and knew a dangerous man. This one wouldn't talk; if you pressed him, you might find trouble.

He shrugged, moved to serve other customers.

Slocum, his elbows on the bar, felt the punch of the booze, and he slouched, as if he hadn't a care in the world.

"Haven't seen you before, cowboy. Jest ride in?" said a voice next to him. "Scotty's the name."

Slocum looked at him, a black-haired, hatchet-faced cowboy in worn denim, with honest brown eyes.

"Yeah, just rode in from Cody."

"Cody, huh? Heard about a stray bunch of braves actin' mean. Run into anything out there?"

"Nothin' special." Slocum pulled a cigarillo. "What about here?"

Scotty grinned. "A little shootin'. We had a rambunctious cowboy, Charlie Denvers, pull his gun."

Slocum puffed his cigarillo. A dumb cowboy, with a snootful of whiskey, got cocky, fightin' mad, pulls his gun.

"Nothin' special 'bout that," Slocum said.

Scotty's hatchet face grinned fiercely. "But Charlie made the mistake of pickin' on Willie James. That special enough? He got shot down by two men in the bunch. Jest like that. Poor Charlie never knew what hit him."

Slocum's jaw hardened. He waited for more, but Scotty just lifted his glass and drank.

"Then what?" Slocum asked.

"Then nothin'. They jest dragged Charley off, potted him in boot hill."

Slocum scowled. "Not much of a town, to let a thing like that happen."

Scotty stared hard. "What d'ye mean, mister?"

"To let a shootin' like that happen. And do nothin'."

Scotty looked astonished. "I'm tellin' you it was *Willie James with a pack of his men, all killers*. Oh, yeah, it was a rotten deal for Charlie, but what could a cowboy do?"

"Shoulda done something," Slocum said.

Scotty's brown eyes squinted. "Well, you're one nervy cowboy. If you're so fired up about it, there's still a chance to put your gun where your mouth is. See that man at the card table, black hat. Name of Biggers. He and the man next to him, name of Snouts, they did the shootin'."

Slocum's gaze swept the saloon. "Any other of Willie's men still here, Scotty?"

Scotty shrugged. "I saw them go—four men and the

filly." He scowled. "Beautiful young filly. Just a damned shame to see a purty thing like her with them outlaws."

Slocum stared at him, shook his head, then to Scotty's amazement started for the card table.

The rawboned man with the hawk nose looked up from his cards, a leisurely look, his eyes sharp. He said nothing. The other three men paused in their play also to look.

"Can you use another player?" Slocum asked politely.

The dealer, a snout-nosed, red-faced man, studied him with a stony look. He, too, said nothing. He wore a black shirt, a wide-brimmed black hat with a bowler top.

"Got money to lose?" said the third player, a square-faced cowboy with steady blue eyes.

Slocum nodded. "I got money, but don't aim to lose it."

"Sit down," said the hawk-nosed one. "My name is Biggers." He pointed to the snout-faced man. "That's Snouts." Shorty was the cowboy with blue eyes, Dan Brown was the fourth man.

"What's the name?" asked Snouts.

"Slocum. John Slocum."

Biggers nodded. "Heard of you, Slocum."

"Nothin' good, I reckon," Slocum said. "Where you from, Biggers?"

"Dodge City."

Slocum watched Snouts shuffle the cards. Biggers seemed to be winning.

"Could I ask how you happened to hear 'bout me?" Slocum asked as he picked up his cards.

Biggers nodded. "You got a rep, Slocum. I knew some

Rebs in Fort Worth. One night, 'round a fire, we got to braggin' what we'd done in the War. And this one Reb, who came from Georgia, said the best sharpshooter he ever saw was Captain John Slocum of the Georgia Regulars. This Slocum, he said, would park himself in the thick of the fightin', and cool as a coot, pick off the bluecoat brass." Biggers smiled. "Guess you're one hotshot with a rifle."

Slocum's face did not change. "May one ask what was that Reb's name?"

"Lee Browne."

Slocum nodded. "I knew him. A good soldier. Whatever happened to him?"

Biggers rubbed his chin to hide a slick smile. "Ran into a hard bullet during a card game. Too much booze, I reckon." He picked up his cards. "He was a sharpshooter like you, with a rifle. But jest a mite slow with a gun." He grinned broadly. "Never can tell how fast a man is till he's pulled his gun. Gimme three cards, Snouts."

Slocum's face was grim, convinced that Biggers had thrown that hard bullet. "That's a might smart thing to say—man is good as his draw. I'll keep it in mind." Slocum looked at his cards. He had two queens. He bet modestly. Snouts tried to bluff him out, but he stayed and two queens won.

"You don't bluff easy," said Biggers.

"Reckon not," said Slocum.

In Shorty's deal, he drew an ace and a jack.

Then Snouts said, "Where you ridin' in from, Slocum?"

"From Cody. I'm lookin' for a man."

They all stayed in and bet, and Snouts pushed the betting. He threw away one card. Then he said, "Who might that be?"

"Willie James, I'm looking for Willie James."

Everyone looked at him. Biggers's lip was tight. "Mighty dangerous man to be lookin' for."

"Yeah," Slocum said.

"Why are you lookin' for him?" said Snouts.

"To blow his head off, I reckon," Slocum said, and picked up the cards dealt him. He filled his glass, but didn't drink, then looked at his draw—ace, three, and ten. He had a pair of aces.

The players were not looking at their cards, just at Slocum.

Biggers took the cigarillo from his mouth. "You got nerve, Slocum. I gotta hand it to you. Nobody ever got a good shot at Willie James. And he's been hunted by some of the best guns in the Territory."

Slocum nodded. "Yeah, he's a hard man to find. Always seems to be runnin'."

Snouts's voice went cold. "I wouldn't say that."

"No, I'm saying it, little fella. He knows I'm trackin' him, but he keeps on runnin'. Usually leaves someone behind to do his dirty work. Dirty, you know what I mean?"

"No," said Biggers. "What d'ye mean?"

Slocum shrugged and casually looked up from his cards. "Now I hear tell, just now, some cowboy came up to Willie, invited him to a fair fight. Willie never pulled his gun. Just two lowdown polecats did it. They weren't even in the line of fire." He smiled at Biggers.

"Don't take much guts to shoot a man who's not facin' you, does it?"

The men watching the game began to edge back, and their movement sent a signal to the bar drinkers; everyone went silent. Attention focused at the card table where, the men sensed, excitement was about to happen.

Biggers looked pale. He hadn't expected Slocum to make a frontal attack. It was a bit unnerving. Slocum had to know he was facing two guns, but it didn't seem to slow him down. It looked crazy for him to push it, almost suicidal, Biggers thought, and he glanced at Snouts who was watching Slocum like a hawk. This was the showdown. There was no way out, Biggers was thinking. The original plan had been to invite Slocum into the game, accuse him of cheating. Snouts would accuse him, Biggers shoot him. Nobody would dare question it. But Slocum seemed to figure the angle and he had headed them off with his tough talk.

Snouts put his cards down, thinking it was a stinking situation. Slocum had to be fast or he wouldn't have taken this route. But no matter how fast, Snouts was thinking, Slocum could not beat two guns. And he'd been talking at Biggers. It meant he would go first for Biggers. Snouts figured he just had to find the right moment. He stared at Slocum: green-eyed, lean, cool, seemingly casual. He looked plenty mean. Well, all it took was a fast bullet. Then he heard Slocum, still talking at Biggers.

"Didn't you say you came from Dodge City?"

"Yeah, I said it."

"Isn't that where that slimy Willie James comes from?

Wouldn't surprise me if you were in that bunch of killin', robbin' polecats." Slocum didn't have to push back from the table. He was already the right distance.

Biggers, the sweat gleaming on his skin, stared at Slocum. He could tell he would be Slocum's target, not Snouts. Well, that was how the cards fell. You couldn't take language like this without pulling your gun. He just hoped Snouts would pull first. He was smart enough to play it that way; he'd done this before.

That was how the play started. Snouts, feeling secure because Slocum was talking and facing Biggers, pulled first, got his gun out of the holster when the whiskey in Slocum's glass hit his eyes. He went blind, heard two shots, never pulled his own trigger. When he finally wiped the whiskey away, he saw Biggers down, a bullet through his head, and Slocum with his Colt pointed at him, the green eyes cold as ice. "Drop the gun, Snouts."

Snouts dropped it.

Slocum leaned forward. "Now, talk real honest, Snouts. Where were you going to meet Willie after you got rid of me?"

"Don't know what you mean." He looked down at Biggers, dead, his eyes glaring.

Slocum put his gun against Snouts's head. "I let you live, you polecat. Don't make me sorry."

"Fork at Red River," Snouts said, and his eyes gleamed viciously.

Slocum nodded, picked up the gun from the floor, and put it in his belt. "Wasted a drink," he said, and poured one into his empty glass, drank it, stared hard at Snouts. "Don't try anything smart," he said, and walked casually toward the door. From the corner of his eye, he saw Snouts move. It was smooth and fast as he reached into Shorty's holster and brought up the gun. In one lightning move, Slocum wheeled and fired. Snouts hurtled back as the bullet ripped into his chest. He dropped near Biggers.

Slocum shrugged at the bartender. "You know, I had a pair of aces, would've won that last pot." He went out the batwing doors.

Willie stared into the long distance at the canyons, giant structures of red rock, vast and dazzling, as if made by some mysterious divine hand, but Willie didn't see their majestic beauty. He saw just a dusty, empty trail where he expected instead to see two horsemen, Biggers and Snouts.

He had given them two extra hours of precious daylight, and now he was ready to give them up. They would not come. Ever. He knew it in his bones. And the reason was clear: Slocum. Somehow Slocum had managed to outfox two good men—Biggers, a fast gun, and Snouts, a crafty polecat.

Willie lit a cigar. He had grievously underestimated Slocum. It had been a mistake. He remembered Slocum's warning at the time they had the rope around his neck. "You're makin' a bad mistake," he had said. Even then, just a minute before death, he had been cool as ice, and he was giving a warning. Willie cursed inwardly, and again he stared down the long trail, hoping to see Biggers, hoping that his premonitions about Slocum would suddenly prove false. But the trail stayed empty and he knew somehow that Biggers and Snouts were starting to push up daisies back in boot hill.

It just meant that Slocum had outsmarted them. They were fast guns, but they weren't foxy. And it was better to be foxy than fast, Willie knew. Slocum would keep coming; it was his nature. Once in a great while, Willie James met a man like Slocum, steely-eyed, with iron in his heart, a man who, once wronged, never gave up the struggle until his last breath. If such men were fast guns, too, then they could be deadly opponents. But you could defeat such men. You outfoxed them, you set traps.

Willie smiled. He knew something about traps. He thought about Tucson, the bank at Tucson. He had to keep in mind that the bank was the real target, and not let his mind get sidetracked. Slocum, if you thought about it, was just a nuisance, a pesky, stubborn nuisance, and it was dumb to exaggerate him, make him all that deadly. One bullet at the right time, right place, suddenly made a deadly man dead. He'd work out a scheme to get rid of Slocum, at the proper time. He had to remember that he'd sent out word to the bunch to meet at Tucson. He could still count on Tom, Burt, and Mike, three good men with guts and guns and loyalty. They were all to rendezvous at the saloon in Tucson. They had to be on their way.

# 6

Slocum looked at the clouds, dark, glowering, burdened with rain. It was just over them, and it would hit in ten minutes. He studied the land for shelter. Against a batch of rocks half a mile to the west he saw the shack. He jerked a thumb at the sky. "We best make a run for shelter."

"And where's that?"

"It's there, that shack stuck in the corner of nowhere. We better go hard for it, those clouds are gonna bust wide open."

She frowned. "Wipe out Willie's tracks?"

"We know he's headed for Tucson. We'll pick him up there."

"Why's he headed there?"

Slocum shrugged. "It's where the money is. Easy to figure a mind like Willie's."

She scowled. "Not that easy."

Slocum glanced at her; she sure had a mysterious rage against Willie, and he wondered when she would open up about it.

The clouds scudded fast, and though they rode hard, they got hit by a torrent before they reached the shack. Slocum pulled the horses under a wooden shed while Diana ran for the door. It had a small stove, a table, two chairs, and a wooden bed; not much of a shack, but it kept out the rain.

Diana's shirt and Levi's were drenched. After a few tries, Slocum got the stove going, and when the fire began to crackle, he pulled off his wet shirt. Diana looked at his bare, muscled chest and turned away.

"Better get outa those things," he said. "Won't do to sit around wet and get sick, 'specially now that we're getting close to the polecat."

She looked hesitant, then saw a beat-up blanket on the bed. "I s'pose so. Just turn around."

"Why?" he asked, all innocence.

She flashed him a look. "I'm getting outa this wet stuff. Are you planning to stare at me?"

He gazed at the wet shirt clinging to her bosom, showing the nipple imprint. Pity, he thought, that she's going to cover all that. He felt stirrings in his groin and decided that when they reached Tucson, somehow he'd get hold of a saloon woman, so that while he traveled with Diana he could keep himself on a low burn.

He grinned, facing the wall. "It's against my worst instincts."

Diana couldn't help smiling It was an intimate situation and she felt its excitement. He had a hard, muscled body, broad at the shoulders, slim at the waist; he was a fascinating man, but she had other things in mind. No time for games; she had an obsession: Willie James

She slipped out of her wet shirt and Levi's, hung them on the string near the stove, and glanced at her naked, curving body. As she threw the scratchy blanket over her smooth skin, she felt a strange excitement being here, practically naked with this powerful stranger, Slocum, whose life she had saved, and who, in return, had saved hers. He was a real full-blooded man.

"It's all right now," she said.

He turned, looked at her, but said nothing. She wondered what he could be thinking, seeing her in this ugly blanket, and was almost sorry that she'd decided not to keep on her wet clothes.

Half a mile away, three horsemen who had been riding in the downpour stopped to stare at the shack up against the rocks. They were hard-faced, bulky, dangerous-looking men.

"I figure we ought to get out of this wet crap and dry out over there," said one rider. He had shrewd gray eyes in a weathered face and wore a curling black hat with a string tied under his chin.

"I don't know, Burt. Willie is waitin' for us in Tucson. He won't like it much if we're late," said the rider in a red flannel shirt. "You know Willie. He's got somethin' planned."

"We don't know if he's got there yet, Tommy," said Burt, smiling. He was a man who smiled a lot, which was strange for a man as dangerous as he. "Willie might be hunkered down somewhere, too, waitin' out the rain."

He glanced at the sky. "Though it might not be rainin' in Tucson. What d'ye think, Mike?"

Mike, a dour, scowling man with a fierce red scar on his cheek and eyes like glittering black stones, shrugged. "He don't like to get wet, just like us."

Burt gazed at the cabin. "They got a warm fire goin'. See the smoke? We could dry off." He grinned. "Might be a purty filly there cookin' for all we know, hey, Mike?"

Mike scowled; he didn't like to be teased about his feelings about women. He also didn't like Burt doing the bossing. He had some hard ideas about that.

"No filly this far out. You're sorta dreamin'," said Tommy.

Burt scowled. "We gotta keep outa trouble. And that's an order. Willie's tryin' to put the bunch together again. If we get into side raids, it ain't gonna happen. Whoever's in there, we jest behave. Get dried off and get out when the rain's gone. Agreed?"

Tommy nodded. "Won't be anyone but a coupla dragged-out ole miners, looking for gold."

"Then let's go," said Burt and smiled, as if the world was a place for jokes.

They rode toward the shack.


Because they were wanted men, they were in the habit of moving with care, and long before they reached the shack they dismounted and crept forward on the crouch. The pounding rain smothered their sounds until Burt, gun in hand, broke open the door, followed by Tom and Mike. Slocum, when he heard the door move, wheeled, gun in hand. If there had been one man, he'd have fired, but three men with drawn guns made bad odds. He held his fire.

"Drop the gun," Burt said.

Slocum dropped it and Burt put it in his gunbelt.

Slocum looked at the men, guessed them to be outlaws. He'd seen too many not to know. And the way they looked at Diana, especially the man with the scar, put him on edge. If they were outlaws and wanted a woman, they'd kill him as soon as look at him.

He smiled at Burt, who he sensed to be the leader.

"Sorry I pulled the gun. Never know who's gonna bust in. But I see you're pilgrims, just as we, caught in the damnedest storm, and lookin' for shelter. We got a good fire goin' and you're welcome to dry out, stay as long as you want, share our grub. This lady is Miss Diana, owner of the Bar M Ranch."

His easy warmth caught Burt by surprise. He stared hard at Slocum; he was big, lean, and muscled, and looked like he could be mighty dangerous. But without a gun, nobody was dangerous, Burt thought. He'd decide what to do with him later. He looked at the filly and almost licked his lips. She was a real lady, not a saloon queen, in spite of wearing that mangy blanket. And this cowboy had introduced her as a ranch owner. Interesting.

"What's your handle, mister?" Burt asked.

"Slocum, John Slocum."

Burt looked at his men. They still had their guns out and were looking at Diana, especially Mike, who always seemed to have a hell of a hunger for women.

Burt stared cold-eyed at Mike. "It's mighty neighborly, Slocum, for you to ask us to share your fire and vittles. Don't mind if we set around and dry out with you. Jest stopped to get outa that blasted rain."

Mike stared at him, his scarred face screwed up with disbelief. "What's all this, Burt?"

Burt glared. "I'm telling Slocum, here, we'll be glad to dry out, and be here with this lovely lady, owner of the Bar M ranch. And that we're gonna be neighborly as hell. Is that clear, you knucklehead?"

Mike's eyes narrowed; he was through taking bullshit from Burt, but not ready to act. Mike figured it this way: he saw the woman, and that was what he wanted. He saw Slocum, a dangerous man to be knocked out. And here was Burt, who understood these things just as he did, yet holding off. Why? Because the lady had a ranch? Maybe Burt figured there was money in the lady. Well, to hell with the money. He stared at Diana, a real beauty. He felt the lust, and his eyes glittered.

Then he heard Tom, his voice hard. "That's right, Mike. We're all gonna set around a while and dry out. That's what we're gonna do. Now, why'n't you light up some tobacco and relax."

Mike's jaw clamped. They'd ganged up on him, and there was nothing he could do. But he could be crafty. He slipped his gun into his holster.

"Any whiskey here?" he asked.

Burt, who'd been watching him with hard eyes, smiled, and put his gun into its holster, as did Tom.

"I'll get some," said Tom, and he ran out into the rain to his horse and dug a whiskey bottle and two tin cups out of his saddlebag. In the house, he stomped his wet boots, poured the cup a quarter full.

"I'll take that," Mike said. "I need it more than you, boy." He drained it, and grinned devilishly. "Good for a wet day. Dries you on the inside." He poured another, drank it, grinned happily, then poured a third and offered it to Diana. "Keep you feelin' good when the weather's rotten."

Diana hesitated, glanced at Slocum, then took the cup. Mike stroked the fiery scar on his face and smiled. It gave him a satanic look. Burt's gray eyes were somber; he didn't like Mike drinking like that. He took a swig from the bottle, passed it to Tom, who poured some into the cup, then passed the bottle to Slocum. "Looks like you could use it."

Slocum shrugged. He didn't like anything about this setup, especially with Diana sitting there wearing nothing but a blanket. A stinking situation. He studied Mike, the fiery scar on his face, probable souvenir of a knife fight, and the baleful black eyes that gazed hungrily at Diana. He looked at her like a starved wolf at a rabbit, ready to spring at any moment. He was the wild card in the deck, and Burt knew it and seemed to want to keep a hold on him. But why, Slocum didn't yet figure. Outlaws could become animals when women came into the picture. At this moment they were doing nothing, drying out, drinking, but when the booze hit their brains all hell might break loose.

"Drink up, Slocum," Mike said, grinning. "It's a short life."

Slocum nodded. "Yes, a short life." As he took a swig, he thought, *Shorter for some than others*. He liked Burt, the way he set down the rules, the way he tried to keep a rope on Mike. Was it possible to get out of this without damage? Three outlaws, a beautiful naked woman, and booze, a dynamite mix. Someone would explode and

Mike was it. And they'd try to get a bullet in him. Because an attack on a respectable woman was a hanging affair. But men like these had piled up enough crimes to be hanged a dozen times.

They had not tied him up, figuring he had no gun, and they could take care of him any time.

The men sat near the stove and Mike peeled his shirt, put it on the string next to Diana's Levi's, and grinned at her. He seemed to find the touch of their clothing exciting, a hint of the intimacy he had already pictured in his mind.

Burt seemed a bit tense, as if something was eating on his mind. "How long do you figger this bad weather?" he asked.

"'Bout an hour or two," Slocum said.

"There's no hurry," Mike said, swilling another cup of booze.

Burt glared at him. "We're tryin' to get to Tucson, not sit and rot in this shack."

"We'll get there," said Mike.

"Willie don't like to be left waitin'," said Tom.

Slocum stared at him. *Willie!*

"No, he don't," said Burt.

Mike shrugged. "Don't need us that bad. If he's got somethin' in mind, he can do it without us."

Burt scowled. "He's countin' on us, and we count on him. Don't ever forget it, Mike."

Mike glowered. "Look, it's rainin' cats and dogs right now. Nothin' we can do, right? We got a nice warm fire. Got some good company. Let's just relax." He swilled another cup of booze and smacked his lips. "Where you folks headed?" he asked Diana.

She ignored him.

"Tucson," said Slocum.

"What business ya got there?" asked Burt.

Slocum smiled slowly. "Never been to Tucson. See what we can find there."

"Like cattle?" asked Tom.

Slocum shrugged. "Could be. What about you men?"

Mike laughed. "We're gonna try to find somethin' in Tucson, too. Gold."

Burt glared at him. "You got a loose tongue, Mike."

"What the hell's the difference, Burt?"

Slocum realized his danger. They were after the bank money in Tucson, and Willie had to be Willie James. These men were part of his bunch, meeting Willie and his boys for the bank job. The danger was, if Mike spilled too much, these men would take hard measures to stop anyone from interfering with their plans.

Slocum gritted his teeth. It was a bitch of bad luck they had run into some men from Willie's bunch. But good luck that these men didn't yet know that Willie wanted him dead. It gave him a slim chance. Mike was the main gunpowder in this hut. If he talked too much, it would force Burt's hand. Slocum felt his position would get suddenly miserable. Until now he presented no threat, but Mike wanted to spill the beans, that the bunch intended to rob the bank. Once Mike did that it would give him the chance to use his gun against Slocum and start the fun with Diana. Mike was a slick devil, and Slocum felt his time was very short.

"Where's your ranch, Miss Diana?" Burt asked with a genial smile.

"Two miles north of Cody," she said. Up to now Diana

seemed to be cool, but Slocum could sense the strain. These men had barreled into the shack at the worst possible time, when she had nothing on but a beat-up blanket, and could not reach her gun. They were outlaws, she sensed, and Mike was some kind of a wolf; she felt almost dirtied when he looked at her with his fiery scarred face and lustful grin. He was the sort of man you'd want to kill rather than yield your body to. It was a terrible setup, she felt, because Slocum, whom she had depended on, was helpless without his gun. These were three desperadoes, good with guns. She sensed that Burt and Tom would be no trouble, and would go on to Tucson. They had mentioned Willie, and it had to be Willie James. She hoped that once the storm passed they would just go on their way, but she had small hope. Mike was a ravening wolf, and he could be counted on to start the fireworks. What could she do? If only she could get to her gun.

"She's a rich young rancher," Mike said with a smirk. "Isn't that nice."

"Yeah, it is," said Burt. "But she's lucky."

"Why?" asked Mike.

"'Cause we ain't got time to mess with it. We gotta meet Willie."

"Are you thinkin' of lettin' her go?" said Mike.

"We ain't got time for her, I tole you," Burt said, and smiled.

Mike's lips tightened. "We gonna *make* time for her."

Tom turned to Slocum. "What about him?"

Mike pulled his gun.

"Hold it," said Burt. "We don't need a killin' and a rapin' here. We got a job to do in Tucson. I tole you before we got here, we don't want any side jobs."

"We got time for it," said Mike.

"No, we ain't," said Burt.

Mike looked at him, then at Tom. "We ain't ever gonna have a beauty like this again. I think we oughta make time for her. What do you think, Tom?"

"I don't know, Mike," Tom said hesitantly. His mottled face gazed at her. He was thinking of Willie.

Mike strode to Diana and jerked at her blanket.

The men looked at her. Her round full breasts were bare, and a thin chemise covered her thighs.

Mike grinned satanically. "Gonna bypass that, Tommy?"

Tom, faced by that lush female body, licked his lips and looked at Burt. "Whaddya think, Burt? She's all woman." Then he turned to look at Slocum.

Mike suddenly grinned. "S'pose we have a wide-open party? Everyone can have a good time." He squinted at Slocum. "I reckon you been lustin' for the lady. Mebbe you'll get a piece, but you just do like we tell you, or I'll put a bullet up your tail."

A red spot appeared on Slocum's cheek, but he did nothing. His rage was overwhelming. But he couldn't yet see the moment. He glanced at Diana; she was standing like a statue, and he couldn't bear to look at her eyes.

Then Burt, who was made of sterner stuff, said, "There's plenty of women in Tucson. This is a decent woman. I don't like the idea."

"No woman is decent," snarled Mike. "Lemme show you." He turned his gun on Diana, opened his Levi's. His organ showed ponderously. "Come to me, honey," he crooned, "I gotta big surprise for you." Burt cursed

and suddenly Mike wheeled and shot him, then turned
to shoot Slocum, but Slocum had already slipped behind
Tom, his hand gripping Tom's body like steel, holding
it in front of him as, with his other hand, he pulled Tom's
gun from its holster. Mike didn't hesitate a moment; he
tried to shoot through Tom to hit Slocum. But it didn't
work. Slocum felt Tom's body jerk as the bullet went
into him, and he triggered Tom's gun, which spit fire
and bullets at Mike. He caught them in his groin and his
torso, which twisted fiercely. He fell to his knees, staring
with violent eyes at Slocum, struggling mightily to bring
up his gun, falling face down, firing into the floor.

There were three dead men in the shack.

Diana stared at them with disbelieving eyes. Then, in
a surge of feeling, she ran up to Slocum, grabbed him
for a full minute, until she became aware of her nudity.

Slocum's face flushed and he felt a rush of passion.
He turned from her and walked out the door into the
rain, let it beat against him for a few minutes until the
passion her body had aroused started to diminish. Then
he went back in.

The men lay there, sprawled in death, blood staining
their shirts and flowing down to the floor.

Diana had slipped on her Levi's and was facing him.

"I'm sorry," she said, "I got carried away."

He nodded. "If you do that again, you better mean
it," he said.

He dragged the bodies behind the hut and dug a pit.

Not long after, the rain clouds scudded south and the
air was moist but clear.

He turned to her, smiling. "I hear Willie James is in

Tucson, planning to rob a bank. We can't let a man like him get rich. He seemed to be expecting these men. We'll have to tell him they ain't gonna make it."

# 7

The Tucson bank, a strong one-story building, was set between the post office and the saloon. Willie James, standing in the hot, dusty street, wearing a false beard, gazed at the bank fondly. The sight of a bank actually gave him a tingling sensation. It was not only the thought of the money in it. He liked money, of course, as much as anyone, but breaking into the bank meant the pleasure of solving a riddle, knocking off a problem. To Willie bank robbing was a game. The bank had the prize and they set traps up to protect it. What fascinated Willie was to spring the traps and grab the prize. Money, of course, was the main thing, but nothing pleased Willie more than thinking about how to do it, then watching it get done.

Willie James knew he had notoriety as a robber, and there might be someone in Tucson who would recognize

him. If that happened, the game would be dangerous.
But Willie had to see the bank layout, and he could trust
nobody's eyes but his own. He scouted in a false beard
and gray denim and black boots. His aim was to be
inconspicuous. He had left the bunch about two miles
out of town and now, alone on the main street, he was
looking at the saloon. He felt a powerful thirst for whiskey, but he gritted his teeth. When on a job, he kept an
iron discipline on himself.

He walked into the bank, cashed a five-dollar bill,
and walked out. No point hanging around. He'd seen
what he wanted: the banker, a hefty, broad-faced man
with cold gray eyes, the yellow-haired teller, two muscular guards. It looked like a bank with money; they got
payroll money for miners and cattlemen. To nail it would
be a challenge.

He rode back to the bunch, found them sitting around
a fire drinking coffee.

Willie sat with them, poured coffee out of the iron
pot into his tin cup. "I been to the bank," he said, "and
tomorrow when it opens in the morning, we're gonna
walk into it, and if all goes well, walk out with a coupla
sacks of money."

Belle's eyes glittered when she heard that; she found
it strangely exciting. She had begun to think that, until
now, her life had been flat and boring, but that Joady
and Willie seemed to make exciting things happen. Still,
part of her stayed wary, and the thought of Diana sobered
her down.

She said, "If you're gonna do bank robbin', I think I
better be somewhere else."

"Oh, no," said Willie, "you're gonna be the star attraction."

She stared at him.

"What d'ya mean, Willie?" Joady was frowning.

"The little lady is goin' into the bank to cash a ten-dollar bill along with you, Joady, her lawful wedded man. Then Belle suddenly groans, grabs her gut, and faints. You can do that, Miss Belle, can't you?"

"I could, but why should I?"

"So we can pick up mebbe a whole lotta money."

"And how will that happen?" she demanded.

Willie smiled casually, took out a cigarillo, and slowly lit it. "The main thing in bank robbin', little lady," he said, "is to get the men who are watching the money to watch somethin' else. Like when a fox throws a false scent, the hounds go the wrong way. So, when a beautiful filly faints in the bank, and her man, Joady, explains she's gonna have a baby, then the men guarding the money lose their concentration. And we'll be there to punish them for that. I'll come in, wearing my marshal badge to make them feel extra safe. And when they gather 'round to help a pretty lady in trouble, me and Joady will be inside the bank persuading the banker to open the safe and share his money. Ketch, you'll be outside with Burt, Tom, and Mike, who should be along any time now." He stood up and stared into the distance. "I sent word for them to meet us here. Looks like a storm over to the east, and it may have stopped them." He ground his teeth. "Don't know what the hell's been happening. I'm trying to get the ole bunch together again, but ain't nobody showing." He turned to look at Belle.

"So what about it, little lady?"

Belle had to admit to herself she found the idea exciting, but still she was a touch fearful. "If it doesn't work, I may end up in prison."

"You may end up a rich young lady, since we share and share alike."

Joady grinned. "You jest say we forced you."

"I'm not sure I should do it," she said.

Willie looked at Joady.

Joady grimaced. "She'll do it."

She stared hard at him. "What makes you so all-fired sure?"

He took her hand, pulled her with him into the bushes about thirty yards from the others.

"Joady," she said.

"Hush up. I'm gonna make you a happy girl." He unbuttoned his trousers and she stared at his excitement, felt her knees go weak. He came close, loosened her shirt, and her breasts came out. He fondled the nipples and she felt a surge of pleasure. She looked up at his darkly handsome, smiling face, her eyes glowing.

He pressed his naked flesh against her groin and she felt herself melting. Belle had discovered something about herself, that she was a young woman of wild passions. She found it thrilling to be tangled up with men like the Willie James bunch, who did daring, terrible things, who lived on the edge of excitement, who never knew from hour to hour if they'd be alive or dead. She was young, yes, but this was life of the highest excitement. It might be a dangerous life, even a short one, but it would never be dull.

Joady loosened her Levi's and they fell to her knees.

He pulled them off, bent to put his mouth between her thighs. He did such marvelous things that she saw stars, and her body quivered. When he came up, strong and lusty, she was ready to do anything he wanted. He made her body go off like dynamite.

Afterward he smiled and said, "It sho' would please me if you went with us into the bank tomorrow, Belle."

She gazed at him, stars in her eyes. "I reckon I'll go with you anywhere," she said, thinking it was crazy, but she had just made Joady, a notorious bank robber, the man of her life, her destiny.

Belle sauntered into the bank, her nerves humming with excitement, and she liked the feeling. Joady came in behind her. They looked like a nice couple come to make a deposit, maybe get a loan. Two hefty guards in blue wearing Colts scrutinized them; the younger guard smiled at the apple-cheeked young beauty, while the grizzled older one squinted at Joady.

The banker, a man called Curtis, was at his desk, frowning over a document, and Jess, the teller, a yellow-haired young man, was talking to a ruddy-faced cattleman.

Belle gushed a bit at Joady, saying they'd have to stop at the general store to pick up sundries. Then she groaned, held her gut, and fell in a dead faint. It was a fine piece of acting just as Willie, wearing his marshal's badge, was coming in the door.

The young guard who'd been fascinated by Belle hurried toward her, and Joady, embarrassed, mumbled that his wife was expecting. The grizzled older guard smiled and came to look down at Belle, prettily sprawled out.

Willie, as the marshal, took command, told him to bring a chair. When the guard turned to do that, Willie pulled his gun. Joady stuck his gun into the belly of the young guard.

Furious at the deception, the guard went for his holster, and Willie hit his hand, sending the man's Colt skittering on the floor.

Willie pointed his gun at the others. "Jest stay easy and nobody gets hurt. It's only money. Don't want to get all bloodied up jest for money, folks."

Belle got up from the floor, and Joady took the sack she had been holding and walked behind the counter where Curtis had been watching, his face pale.

"Jest open the safe, mister."

Curtis ground his teeth. "Dirty trick, using that saucy filly."

"Reckon so, but a smart trick, too. Gets us to the money," said Willie, grinning.

"Who the hell are you?" growled the banker.

"The name's Willie James, and we got no more time. You men face the wall," he told the guards. Though they scowled, they turned. Willie stood close behind them, then nodded at Joady, who put his gun at the banker's head. "Jest open the safe, mister."

"You won't get away with this, Willie James. They're gonna bust your bunch once and for all."

"You got five seconds to decide if it's the money or your life, mister," said Joady.

Curtis looked at his guards with disgust. "All right," he said.

His blue eyes in a tight squint, he opened the safe and turned around with a gun. Joady shot him, and he spun like a top and fell, blood leaking from his mouth.

"Damn," said Willie. "Move fast. Belle, you get out to Ketchum and the horses. Anyone comin' jest say it was accident gunfire."

Joady scooped up two bags of money and dropped them into the sack. He came alongside Willie, who was standing behind the guards, and quickly they slugged the men with their pistol butts. The men dropped. Willie turned to the teller and the cattleman. "You're still breathin'. Jest stay easy, right there."

They walked casually through the door and closed it.

Outside, two men and a woman in a yellow bonnet, curious about the gunshot, were walking toward the bank. Ketchum was on his horse, alongside Belle. He smiled and lifted his gun. "Jest turn and keep on walkin', folks. It's good for your health."

The lady in the bonnet didn't quite understand, so Willie, who swung over the horse held for him by Ketchum, said courteously, "The bank is closed, ma'am, on account of lack of funds."

They rode at an easy canter out of town, then dug in their spurs.

For almost half an hour, they rode steadily through wild country, past gullies and arroyos, under a brassy sky. The red rock canyons soared with mighty grandeur. They stopped finally in a pocket of small boulders.

With his soiled red neckerchief, Willie mopped his broad-boned face. "Let's jest see what we got here." There was new money in the open bags. "Payroll money," Willie said, smiling. "Not a bad haul. So, let's have some refreshment. We'll count it later."

Over the coffee, Willie grinned at Belle. "You're an

honest-to-goodness actor, Belle. Looked like the real thing, watching you go down like that."

She laughed. It had been thrilling for her from start to finish. She loved the excitement, the danger; it made her blood pump, made her feel alive. She didn't like the killing—that was bad—but living on the edge of such excitement thrilled her to the bone.

Willie stared coldly at Joady. "Why don't you shoot right? I tole you, no killin'."

Joady scowled. "That dog turned with a gun. He wasn't just gonna wave it at me."

"You coulda shot his gun. Or hit his arm. Shoulda been expectin' he might try that trick."

Joady's scowl deepened. "How d'ye know he didn't aim to kill me? Ain't gonna wait to find out." Joady turned to Ketchum. "How come I ain't heard any beefin' from you? You're always ready for that."

"I wasn't there, Joady. I figure you did what you had to. But it's bad business to kill bankers. It was something like that up in Kansas that got folks all riled up and put that posse of long riders on us. And I do remember it was your gun that did it there, too."

Joady looked sulky. "Anyone pointing a gun at me is not planning to do me a kindness. I figger he's shootin' to kill, that it's him or me. And that's the end of it." He turned to Willie. "See how Ketch does it," he said complainingly. "Somehow he faults me."

"It was me that faulted you, Joady. And it's true that it was your gun that brought on the posse." He paused and smiled. "But I reckon that, in your place, I jest might have done the same thing. So let it rest. We'll count the money, and because it's new, we may have to cache it for a time. Start spending it right off won't do at all."

Joady looked at Belle. "Honey, you did a mighty fine job. You're a full member of this bunch. And you get your share of the haul. Am I right, Willie?"

Willie smiled. "Might be. We'll cross that bridge when we get there." He looked at her admiringly. "You sure got a lotta cool nerve for a young filly. Could be you're born for this sorta work."

Belle glowed under their praise. "Beats kitchen work."

Everyone laughed.

The heat blistered the weathered frame buildings of Tucson as Slocum and Diana rode into town. The heat, however, didn't seem to keep people in their houses, and a glance at the excitement in the main street told Slocum that the town had been hit hard, and not too long ago. Four men and a woman were huddled near the bank, talking earnestly, and when they spotted Slocum and Diana, one young man stared at them, suspicion glinting in his eyes.

Slocum turned to Diana. "Looks like Willie has paid his respects to the bank."

"I just hope they didn't drag poor Belle into it."

"Why should they do that?"

"They're dogs, not men, that's why," she said sharply.

They swung off their horses in front of the saloon, tied the reins to the railpost, then sauntered toward the knot of people in front of the bank. Slocum glanced at the yellow-haired man in the black vest who had been watching them with suspicious eyes. He was slender, a bit hunched, and his eyes were red. Ran into sudden misfortune, Slocum thought. In the group was a lady in a yellow bonnet, a brick-faced, muscled cowboy, and an old-timer. When Slocum spoke, he directed his question to the old-timer, who had pale blue eyes and grizzled skin.

"Looks like you've run into excitement around here, partner."

The old-timer grinned. "A peck of excitement. Willie James has given us the honor of his presence."

Slocum glanced at Diana, his mouth tight. "Where's he at?"

The old-timer stared at him, grinning. "Where? He ain't sitting 'round here countin' the money. He's kicked up a lotta dust by now."

Slocum looked disgusted. "So he cracked the bank and got clear away? Just like that. What kinda town is this?"

The grizzled face stared at Slocum with washed-out blue eyes. "Ain't easy to put a lasso on Willie James, mister. But we got a posse out after them desperadoes. That right, Jess?"

The young man in the black vest nodded, and he stared with hard brown eyes at Slocum. "You seem interested in Willie James, mister. Who are you?"

Slocum had been aware during his exchange with the old-timer that runty Jess, for some reason, had been eyeing Diana and himself with a sullen, suspicious face. He seemed to have some wild idea in his head.

"Name's Slocum, John Slocum. This is Diana Keating. We're interested in Willie James. We'd like to nail him to a barn door."

"And why is that?" persisted Jess, suspicion still gleaming in his eyes.

"Why? We got plenty of reasons."

Jess glowered. "Reckon I got more reason. Them robbers shot my Uncle Curtis. Shot him down like a dog."

Slocum rubbed his chin. "Like a dog? Don't sound like Willie James."

"What d'ye mean?" Jess demanded belligerently. "He's a lowdown killer, like the rest of them."

"Did Willie do the killing?" asked Slocum.

Jess glared. "What the hell difference does it make? No, it wasn't him, it was the dark-haired one, the one who came in with the girl, said she was expecting. A dirty trick. That's what Uncle Curtis said, using that girl to trick us."

Slocum glanced at Diana; her face was hard. He turned to Jess. "So you were there? You saw it all."

"Yeah, I saw it all. A mangy bunch of killers, all of them. Includin' the girl." He stared at Diana. "Fact is, first time I saw you I figgered you to be the same girl. But you're older, though you look like her well enough."

"She's my sister," said Diana coldly.

His eyes narrowed. "I figgered you're part of that bunch," he said, as his hand went to his holster.

Then his eyes widened as he found himself looking into Slocum's gun. "Don't do that, little cowboy, if you like breathin'. Now I'll just tell you that we're huntin' Willie James. That he's done us wrong. And he's grabbed her little sister, here, forcin' her to do what the gang wants. She's an innocent young girl, feared for her life, and they're making her do it."

For the first time the lady in the yellow bonnet spoke up. "I saw that girl, no more than sixteen she was. And sister or not, she didn't look like a prisoner. In fact she looked like she was having a big time. Eyes sparkling and smiling ear to ear. Didn't look like no forced girl to me."

"That's the damned truth," said Jess. "The way she faked it, dropping in a faint, took the guards in, and that's why them robbers got the drop. It's a mighty fishy story." He turned to the red-faced, thick-necked cowboy. "Ain't it, Andy?"

The cowboy just shrugged and looked at Slocum with pale blue eyes. Then he said. "You say you got a grievance against Willie James?"

Slocum nodded.

"In that case you can join me. I come to town too late to join the posse, and was aiming to ride and catch up. We might all travel together." He squinted at Diana.

"Mighty kind of you," said Slocum. And he looked expectantly at Jess. After all, he'd lost an uncle.

Jess shrugged. "I'd like nothin' better than to get my hands on that Willie James and his bunch of cowards who shot my uncle. But I hafta stay and do the bank's business."

"Figgered Willie got all your money," Slocum said.

Jess smiled widely. "We're not that dumb. We got secret hidin' places."

Andy pulled his gun. "You're dumber than you look, Jess, talkin' about your hidden money to them. They're in that bunch sure as God made polecats. Now, mister smartass, jest put up your hands. We're going to put you in a safe place till the posse comes back with your friends. If they don't bother to hang 'em first. We're goin' to check out your story, which to my ears is a bunch of hogwash." And he leaned over and snatched Slocum's gun from its holster.

Slocum stared at him in amazement; he'd let this local yokel get his gun, and now was at his mercy. "Listen, you bonehead," he said through gritted teeth, "I'm tryin' to snare Willie James and get back your bank money. You're slowing me down."

"May slow you down to a full stop, you give us any trouble," Andy said. "As for Willie James, he won't go far. We got a five-man posse goin' after him."

Slocum stared disbelievingly at this red-faced, thick-necked cowboy, the stubborn tilt of his heavy chin. "You're dreaming if you think they're gonna nab Willie James. They had a posse of the long riders, some of the best men in Kansas, trying to hunt him down, and never did it."

"That's right," said the old-timer. "They never got him. Our boys are goin' to run into rough times, Andy."

Andy scowled. "I got faith in the boys especially with Sheriff Dustin leadin' 'em. They're gonna hunt down that rotten bunch, bring 'em back, and hang 'em on the highest tree in Tucson. And you better pray they bring 'em back, 'cause, as far as I can see, you're part of the bunch. You're gonna need one of them to prove you're not."

Diana put her hands on her hips and glared. "You gotta be the dumbest cowboy in town. Anyone with an ounce of sense would figger that if we were part of that bunch, we'd be with them, with the money. Why back here?"

Andy scowled, and looked at Jess, who came to his rescue. "Don't you be so damned persnickety, madam, cussin' out decent folks. You two jest got left behind and now are catchin' up to your gang. And how come your sister is workin' with that bunch? That's what Judge Bacon would call evidence that 'incriminates.' He's our travelin' judge and he'll be here soon enough to lay justice on you two, and your robbin', killin' gang."

Andy stared severely. "There. You put it in a nutshell, Jess. Now no more gabbin'. Just start steppin'. The two of you are goin' in the lockup for safe keepin'."

They were locked in two cells of a small jail, where Andy appointed himself jailer. As he told Jess, "I was a-goin' to join the posse, but this is my rightful job till the sheriff gets back."

He clicked the lock on the iron door, sat on the chair, and put his feet on the desk, his hands behind his head.

"Won't be long," he purred, "before your gang joins you in there." And Andy couldn't help congratulating himself on doing a smart piece of work on two desperate characters.

Slocum paced the cell, smoking a cigarillo, cursing this yokel's stupidity and his own tendency to lose his sharp instinct for danger when he mingled with good citizens. The last thing he expected would be some dunce of a cowboy to mistake him for one of Willie's boys. It was, in a sense, Belle who had brought this misfortune down on him and Diana. Her easy liaison with the gang had made Diana and anyone who was with her objects of suspicion.

He shook his head. This put the skids on his pursuit of Willie and gave the bunch the chance of a clear getaway, unless that posse could nail them, which he found hard to believe. Meanwhile, he would just have to stay alert and hope that Andy, who had to be the prize specimen of a mulebrain, would make a slip-up.

A couple of hours dragged by, and they were heavy for Slocum. He sprawled on the iron cot, and through slitted eyes kept a tight watch on Andy, who after an hour began to get restless. Andy was a man who rode the range, and sitting at a desk chafed him. He wandered around the small office, looked at the bulletin board, at the rifle stand, through the window. He soon got bored with everything, then turned to them. "Guess I'm s'posed to feed the prisoners, though it's a waste of food, far as I kin see."

He looked at them hard, to give an impression of toughness. "Don't try anything funny." He grinned, jingled the key in his back pocket, and went out the door.

Diana stared over at Slocum. "How'd we let a numbskull like that grab us?"

"That's how it happens. You don't expect mischief from a law-abiding citizen, but when they're dumb they're the worst."

"What'll we do?" she asked.

He'd been thinking hard about it. Her cell was next to his.

"If you can, get him to come to you at this corner of the cell," he said. "Try to get him to serve the food to you there. If not, think of something."

She nodded, quick to see the possibilities.

"While we're locked up here, I fear Willie's going to lose us," she said.

He shrugged. "He'll have to stop for the posse. If I know his kind, he don't like to keep running."

She said nothing, but looked like she had a lot on her

mind. Probably thinking of Belle, and what kind of mischief she was up to, Slocum thought.

The sun had started down when the front door was unlocked. Slocum watched Andy come in, face flushed from whiskeys at the saloon, where he'd been bragging. He had a package which turned out to be two plates each with a cut of beef and some beans.

"Hell of a thing," he grumbled, "playin' nursemaid to a couple of outlaws." He was about to slip the food under the cell door, when he stopped and looked warily at Slocum standing nearby.

"Move back of the cell, mister. You ain't gonna pull any funny business with me."

"Just hungry, Andy, that's all. Wanta get to the food. We're innocent folk, as you'll find out."

"Yeah, the innocent Jesse boys." Andy grinned. "You look like one of the most wanted outlaws in the Territory. I'll probably get a big reward for your capture. Now move back or I'll blow your head off and say you were trying to escape."

"Plumb loco," muttered Slocum.

Andy shoved his plate under the iron opening of the cell.

Then he did the same to Diana, watched her pick it up and give him a small smile.

"Pity," he said, "a nice-lookin' lady like you gettin' mixed up with this desperado. You made a serious mistake, miss." He turned to stare malevolently at Slocum. "But he musta lured you into this bad life. You, an innocent woman, and him, romancin' you. You shoulda had more sense."

Diana batted her eyes at him as she picked up her

plate. "That's a lot of truth, Andy. That's just the way it happened. Never figgered him to be an outlaw, but I got caught up by my feelings, lost my head. Now look where I am." She began to weep. "You make one mistake, and you get branded for life. Ain't fair."

Andy was amazed. He had hit on the truth of what happened, and here was this lovely young woman spilling tears of regret. It jolted him, embarrassed him. He didn't know what to do. He glared at Slocum, who came forward curiously.

"Don't let that varmint make you cry, Diana, honey," Slocum said, holding the cell bars, looking grief-stricken.

"Shet up," snarled Andy. "It's dogs like you who bring such women to ruin. Oh, you're gonna hang from the highest tree in Tucson, mister." And he came close to Diana's cell, pulling his neckerchief. "Here, miss, dry your eyes. I'm sure the judge will see mitigatin' circumstances in your case. I seen it happen."

Diana took the neckerchief from him, and Slocum took hold of his belt, jerking him hard, bumping his head against the cell bars, stunning him. Then Slocum got an armlock around his neck, holding tight until he felt Andy go limp. He let him drop to the floor and reached into his pocket for the cell key. It took two minutes to get both cell doors open and pull Andy inside the cell, lock it, and put the key in his pocket.

"He should get out by Christmas," Slocum muttered, and peered out the front door. Their horses were still tied to the railpost in front of the saloon. The sun had started down, a quiet time of the day. Just two cowhands were on the street, and the gray old-timer, sitting in a rocker on the porch.

"We'll just walk out easy, and ride out easy. No hurry unless somebody raises a holler," he said.

The grizzled old-timer stared at him and grinned ear to ear. He waved as Slocum and Diana jogged past.

# 8

The trail meandered through a canyon with rocks towering on either side. Willie led his bunch through it, dismounted, and pulled his rifle and field glasses. "Let's double back and climb a bit," he said.

They climbed some rocks, then Willie, using his field glasses, studied the horsemen riding steadily toward them on the trail.

"There's five of them, and they're riding stupid," he said.

"What d'ye mean, stupid?" asked Joady.

"Jest pushin' their horses, not stoppin' to look, jest figgering we're running, and they're goin' to catch up." He smiled grimly.

"They're gonna catch hell," Ketchum said.

Belle looked at Willie. She didn't like the killing part of this adventure.

Willie shrugged. "It's too bad they didn't turn back. Sure gave 'em enough time. We can't let them push us any more. But they're muleheaded. Do they think a small-time posse is gonna catch up with Willie James?" He grinned. "Not even the posse of long riders caught up with us."

He gazed at Belle as he pulled his rifle. "Sorry 'bout it. But we jest can't keep runnin' all the time. Gotta sleep nights."

He pointed to the high boulders on the other side of the trail. "Joady, you go up there. We get them in a crossfire. I'll pick up the first rider, Joady, you get the second, and Ketchum the third. Then all hit the other two." He stared thoughtfully at the five riders, riding hard. "Best go now, Joady."

Belle watched Joady clamber down the heavy big rocks and cross over to the other side of the trail, where she lost sight of him as he climbed up.

Willie squeezed through two tight boulders, trying to get a better sighting of the posse, leaving Ketch and Belle alone.

She glanced at him, a powerfully built man with sandy hair, dark eyes, and a square, bronzed face. He seemed to look at her a lot. He had gentleness, yet she still felt he was a man. She liked him, and wondered what would have happened between her and Ketchum if she hadn't met Joady first.

"Are you afeared?" he asked, smiling.

She shook her head. "Hard to be feared of anything, the way Willie runs things. Seems always to be on top of them."

He grinned. "Willie's smart. Seems always to know where the trouble is and how to head it off." He looked at her pretty face. "But all this trouble, breaking into banks, runnin' from posses—reckon it might be too much excitement for you."

Her violet eyes sparkled. "Ketch, it don't bother me a bit. Fact is, I thrive on it."

He smiled. "You're a gutsy young filly, Belle, and Joady is sure one lucky man." He looked across the trail to the heap-up of boulders from where Joady would be shooting from ambush. "I confess I'm jest not crazy 'bout the way he treats you."

Her lips tightened. "I got no complaint, Ketch."

He stared hard at her. "Don't think you're the kind who makes complaints, even if you had 'em."

Willie came back and glanced from his cousin to Belle. Apparently he had overheard them. "Belle's as pretty as a springtime flower, ain't she, Ketch?" he said.

Belle almost laughed, because Ketch looked tight-lipped, as if he'd been caught with his hand in the cookie jar. "Reckon so," he said finally.

By that time Willie was no longer interested. He looked at his rifle. "Belle, you stay down, keep outa sight, so no stray bullets get to you."

Sheriff Dustin of Tucson on his Appaloosa felt himself riding the whirlwind after the devil. And the devil was Willie James.

From behind he could hear the thundering hoofbeats of his posse as they all galloped past the dry gulch. The sheriff turned for a fast look at his men: Hogan, Merrill, Lemon, and Boone, every one a fine, red-blooded cowboy about to cover himself with glory. They were hot on the heels of the most notorious robber of the Territory, Willie James, and about to run him down.

He pulled at the reins to stop his horse, and his men all pulled up around him, their horses blowing hard.

"I can smell their tails, boys. We're tight on them. They've got no stamina, they're robbers, don't know how to ride, just how to steal. That filly with them is a ball and chain, draggin' on them. Won't be long before we'll have the Willie James bunch roped, branded, and locked in the Tucson jail, ready for hangin'. And you're all gonna be heroes, 'cause Willie is the biggest thievin' rat in the Territory." He pointed to the canyon. "I reckon we'll spot them when we get t'other side of the canyon. We'll jest plumb ride 'em down. Now let's ride like hell."

The sheriff dug in his spurs and his horse spurted forward. His boys whooped and hollered and dug in their spurs, too.

As he rode, the sheriff dreamed a bit. He was closing in on the most famous robber in the Territory, and the way he figured it, there was no way that bunch could get away. Sooner or later he and his posse were going to close in.

Sheriff Dustin heard the wind whistle past his ears. He felt in his bones it was only minutes before he'd come in sight of the bunch, once they crossed the split in the canyon. On the other side of that split, he was dead sure to spot the three thieving polecats and the filly, dragging their asses.

Again he dug in his spurs.

He could almost taste the glory when the rifle bullet hit him. It went through his forehead and took off the back of his skull. He never heard the shots that wiped out his posse. He just died with a dream of glory, which is not a bad way to quit this world.

Belle crouched behind the rocks and watched Willie position himself between two crags that hid him from the coming posse. Ketchum threw her a warm smile which did funny things inside her. Then, holding his rifle carefully, he crawled down, finding a crevice from where he, too, could see clearly.

The minutes began to crawl. Belle crouched quietly, her heart pounding. Something bad was about to happen, and she was in its center. What in hell was she doing here, with these men, outlaws, who were just about to shoot five law-abiding citizens who'd come out to punish these men for robbing?

She tried not to think. Something bad was about to happen, and in part, she'd helped it happen. She must not think about that. She had to remember that she'd committed herself to Joady, and you didn't play fast and loose in this world. You made your choice and stuck with it.

She could hear the muffled sound of hoofbeats, still far, but not too far for a rifle bullet. She looked at the hard, shiny surface of the stone near her, and felt the beat of her heart. There were five citizens racing into a trap, about to be shot to hell. She could warn them just by standing and shouting. Could she do that? Should she? What had she done?

Then she heard the blast of Willie's rifle, its deadly bounce off the canyon. Then Joady's rifle from his hideout across the trail, then Ketchum's.

Silence.

It was over.

She peered from the rocks and saw what she feared: five torn men sprawled on the ground, and five riderless horses running wild.

She shut her eyes and turned away.

Willie came down from his perch, joined by Ketch. They looked out at the sprawled, silent figures.

"Five dumb cowboys," Willie said.

He glanced at Belle and a strange smile came to his face, but he said nothing.

When they all got to their horses, Willie pulled a bottle of whiskey and a cup from his saddlebag, poured a bit into it, and gave it to Belle.

"Didn't like that much, did you, Belle?"

"Not much," she said, and drank the whiskey, which made her feel easier.

Joady stared at her. "What the hell's the matter?"

She was silent.

"Tell them," said Ketchum. "Don't be afraid."

Joady threw him a mean look.

Belle couldn't help sipping a bit more of the whiskey. They watched her.

Finally she said, "It was bloody."

"Had to be," said Willie.

"Couldn't you have fired a warning shot or something?" she asked.

They smiled. Willie pulled out a cigar and lit it. "If we did that, they'd go into hiding. Then it'd be a slow stakeout. They'd send back for more men. Keep us pinned down. Finally they'd get us. String us up, send you to

prison for ten years to come out an old lady. Is that what
you want, Belle?"

He puffed the cigar, blew the smoke at the sky. "Short
and sweet, that's how to do it. They never knew what
hit them." He swilled a mouthful of whiskey from the
bottle. "The fact is, Belle, I'm not one for killin'. Jest
do it in self-defense. All we want is the money."

Joady and Ketchum smiled. Willie put his leg into the
stirrup of his saddle and swung over his horse. "Now,
let's head north."

Slocum picked up the trail easy enough, five men in the
posse tracking Willie's bunch. The trail went into rocky
country, scattered, thick boulders which could give shelter from gunfire.

The sky was a stretch of hot blue and the sun a yellow
blaze. The flanks of the horses glistened with sweat, and
twice they stopped to let the horses drink.

After another hour of tough riding over a twisting,
rocky trail pocketed with parched brush, they stopped to
eat in the shadow of a huge boulder.

Diana was in a dark study, Slocum thought, as he bit
into his jerky. He had an idea of what bothered her, but
said nothing. Finally, when she started drinking coffee,
she said, "Were they telling the truth 'bout Belle, do you
think, Slocum?"

He shrugged. "Why would they lie?"

Diana looked at a soaring buzzard high in the sky.
"So hard to believe," she said slowly. "Little sister working for them. They must have forced her."

"Maybe," he said. It wouldn't be fair for him to make

a judgment, since he'd never met Belle. "The old lady might be reading it wrong," he added gently. "Maybe Belle was smiling to get outa that bank in one piece."

Diana's deep brown eyes gleamed. "Yeah, maybe." She gazed across the rocky land. "There's a bit of the devil in Belle," she said slowly. "Always has been. She craves excitement. That's the kind of girl she is. I have a bad feelin' that she went with Joady because she wanted to. That she enjoys what's happening around her. A touch of the devil, she's always had it. Maybe we can save her from where's she headed. We gotta catch up fast. I'm afraid for her."

Slocum rubbed his chin. "We don't yet know if she's that far gone. It's too quick. A girl can't change overnight. Won't be long before we pick up something. Don't know if that posse's any good." He looked thoughtful. "They're dealing with vultures, men who have helled around for years, killing and robbing. Professionals. I can't put much faith in that posse from Tucson."

She stood up, poured more coffee from the iron pot into her cup, sat down, and gazed at him with gleaming brown eyes. "Slocum, I must tell you, you're one red-blooded man. I'm thinking about what happened in that shack. Mike was the lowest polecat I ever saw. I figgered it was all up with us. I was in despair. Could see no way out. And I was ready to rip that polecat's eyes out if he laid a finger on me. As for you, I figgered you to be a goner. No gun, and them with three guns. Then all of a sudden everything changed. They had the force, and then they were gone. Like a miracle. But, I gotta admit, it was mostly you. You just seemed to know what to do at the right time." She smiled. "Reckon the smartest thing

I ever did was to save your hide from a hanging. Because ever since, you've been saving my hide."

He grinned. "Prettiest hide I ever saw."

She reddened. "I reckon you saw a lot of it, too, back there in the hut."

He bit his lip as his memory brought back the look of her body; he remembered her full breasts, slender waist, full hips, and her flesh pressing against him. Even now the thought sent a surge of excitement to his loins. His face darkened. It was unfair that he had to fight his desires, too, at a time when he needed all his concentration. Tracking the James bunch had to be mighty dangerous. They were, the three of them, a rare bunch of survivors, and there had to be a reason: Willie James. He was smart as a fox, knew a lot of tricks. You couldn't let your guard down for a moment while on his tracks. Oh, Slocum craved Diana, all right, but didn't know, if he made a move, how she'd respond. He was s'posed to be hunting the enemy, he kept telling himself, not sparking her. Yes, he had to keep a tight rein on his feelings or all hell would hit them. He'd seen such things happen. You kiss a lady and get a bullet up your tail. What if he made a pass, and she bypassed: wouldn't it ruin things between them? He could almost hear her say, more in sorrow than in anger, "You got me wrong, Slocum."

No, he had to pass it by. But he promised himself that if and when he reached the next town, he'd grab himself a saloon lady and shoot the works.

Slocum on the trail rode with restless eyes, searching always for the telltale clues of man and beast, for the site of ambush. So when he spotted far ahead the way the trail cut through the canyon, with crags rising on each side to give camouflage for ambush, he alerted, and pulled the reins of the roan. Diana, too, pulled her reins and looked at him.

"What is it?"

He pointed to the canyon. "If I were Willie James with a posse hot on my tail, aiming to hang me, I might take a position up there and try to discourage them." He smiled grimly. "You don't go blind against a site like that."

Diana gazed at the jagged crags glinting innocently in the glaring afternoon sun.

"Doesn't look that menacing to me," she said.

"No, and that's why Willie picked it." His sharp green eyes scrutinized the land.

She looked puzzled. "Did you say he *picked it?* How'd you know that?"

For just a moment he had glimpsed a big-winged bird lift off the ground and settle nearby, out of sight. Slocum pulled a cigarillo from his shirt pocket and lit it. "He picked it, all right, but the posse didn't seem to figure that out. They just smelled a hot trail and tried to run down the James bunch." He sighed. "But it never happened."

Her clear brown eyes gazed at him in wonder. "How do you know all this, Slocum?"

"Caught sight of a buzzard."

"A buzzard." Her face hardened and she looked searchingly at the crags. "You might be wrong. Could be a dead animal."

"It won't be."

Diana looked at his hard, square face, and suddenly believed him. Slocum, she realized, had an uncanny ability to read trail signs and danger. She gazed at the bronzed canyon towering over the trail, and tried to see movement in the jagged rocks. "Would Willie be there now? Maybe waiting for us?"

Slocum puffed his cigarillo. "Reckon not. He's got a lot of money. He won't hang around with that. Just now he's not worrying about us. We're not pushing him. He might even imagine that Biggers and Snouts did their job. No, not till he gets sight of us will he know for sure we're still tracking him."

"Then let's go." She prodded her horse.

Though fairly sure Willie was not lurking behind the crags, Slocum kept a wary eye out for movement. He saw a riderless horse grazing as they rode closer. He glanced at Diana. "Doesn't look good for the posse."

Fifteen minutes more of riding brought them in sight of a flock of buzzards. They'd been at work on the bodies for hours.

He glanced at Diana. Her brown eyes were wide with shock.

"There's nothing we can do here," he said, and slapped the flank of her horse as he himself rode forward.

# 9

Willie James always rode at the head of the bunch. He took that spot not only because he was boss man, but also to protect the bunch. He had found through experience that he sensed danger quicker and figured the angles faster than any of them. He was thinking about this as he rode, his hard blue eyes studying the land.

He was thinking about Belle. A gutsy filly; she had done a smooth job at the bank. She could be useful to the bunch, but... He was thinking, too, how jangled she had looked after the posse ambush; she hated it. It made her realize, real sharp, who she was locked in with: robbers and killers. Willie smiled. She hadn't figured on that when she tumbled for Joady. She had gone for his brawn and the heat in his britches, and now might be brooding on what she'd got into. Such a filly could make

117

the wrong move and wipe them all out. She needed watching.

He pulled his neckerchief and mopped the sweat on his face. The sun was fierce. He glanced at the towering Catalinas stretching west, simmering under that fiery ball in the sky. Tombstone was a couple of hours off; a nice place to lay over.

He pulled out his canteen, guzzled, put it away, and began to think again. He didn't like the way Ketch looked at Belle. Couldn't help bring on fireworks. Joady was a wild bronc, stretched out, ready to go off like a honed trigger. His brother, but not like him at all. More like Mike in the old bunch. What the hell had happened to Mike, to Burt and Tom? Supposed to meet in Tucson, and they never showed. Why? He counted on Burt, a dependable man.

A wild idea sneaked into Willie's head. What if, by some strange chance, they ran into Slocum and Diana? It could have happened; all of them headed for Tucson and bumping into each other. Now, thinking of it, that storm east of Tucson—could their paths have crossed, and if so, what then? The plain fact was that Burt, Tom, and Mike didn't show, and that was not good. This Slocum was one poisonous hombre.

Willie cursed the day they made the mistake of trying to hang Slocum.

Again Willie gazed at the land: brown, red, and pink, and always looming up, the bronze canyons, vast, awesome, terrible, standing like that unchanged since the birth of the earth.

On sudden impulse, he lifted himself on his saddle

and looked back. Far in the distance, very far and very faint, there was dust.

So someone was coming. Someone.

In his bones he knew it was Slocum.

A jackrabbit skidded out of the brush and Ketchum whipped out his gun; the rabbit jumped two feet off the ground.

"Why'd you do that, Ketchum?" asked Joady. "We aim to be eatin' like gentlefolk in Tombstone."

Willie glared at him.

"Well, " said Joady, "we got all this money, we oughta be spendin' some of it."

"That'd be smart, spendin' big, clean money in a small town," said Willie. "We'll camp there in the shadow of that boulder."

It was a massive boulder on a high piece of land giving a view of the valley behind them.

They got a fire crackling, and the rabbit was soon frying in the skillet, the coffee pot boiling. They ate and drank in silence, until Joady shook his head. "Sometimes, Willie, I think you're more interested in the trick of stealin' money than in the spendin' of it."

"There's fun in that, I s'pose," Willie said, and looked at the horizon where, despite the still lingering light, the moon was starting up. "Trouble with the life of bank robbin' is it don't have much of a future. Never heard of a bank robber who died of old age."

Joady grinned. "Not many folk die of old age in the Territory. It's a short life and a merry one." He got up, walked to his saddlebag, and pulled out a bottle of whiskey, then poured some in his coffee and passed the bottle to Willie. "What in hell do you figger happened to Biggers and Snouts? I sure figgered they'd take care of Slocum."

Ketchum took the whiskey from Willie and poured some into his cup. "This Slocum is one hot gun. Don't you think so, Willie?"

Willie just shrugged and drank his coffee.

"And Miss Diana has the best shootin' eye I ever saw," Ketchum said, looking at Belle. "Where'd your sister learn that?"

"Born with it," Belle said, smiling. "She could shoot the eye outa a squirrel when she was in her teens. Dad was proud as a peacock about it. Showed her off to the neighbors."

"Trouble is," said Ketchum, "she's now turnin' that shootin' eye on us. Reckon she'd be tired by now. We come a long way."

"She'd be through long ago," said Joady, "if not for that polecat, Slocum. They come through some mighty rough territory—Apaches."

Willie made a noise in his throat.

Ketchum stared at him, then said thoughtfully, "Whatever happened to Burt and the boys? Were s'posed to meet at Tucson. Though we didn't need 'em after all, it mighta been bad if we didn't catch the town off guard."

Willie nodded. "If you want my opinion. I think Burt and his boys have joined Biggers in boot hill."

Ketchum's eyes narrowed. "Slocum?"

"Jest a feelin'," Willie said. "But I'm willing to bet on it."

Joady grumbled. "You're makin' this Slocum some

kind of a big gun. He's been lucky, is what I say. He coulda been dead as a lynched rat if it hadn't been for that she-devil Diana. Takes one bullet to put Slocum underground."

"Takes one bullet to put anyone underground," said Ketchum.

Belle was puzzled. She hadn't been there when the bunch had tried to hang Slocum. "How'd this cowboy, Slocum, get into all this?"

Willie smiled. "It was your sister. We had a rope around his neck and she shot it off. Ever since he's been houndin' us."

Belle thought a moment. "Why'd she shoot it off? Didn't know him."

"Mebbe she figgered anyone we were tryin' to get rid of could be useful to her," said Willie. "Now they both keep comin'." He lifted the whiskey bottle to his lips, guzzled, then grinned. "She's comin' after you, Belle. Thinks we grabbed you. She doesn't know that it was you who grabbed Joady."

Belle smiled. "Is that what happened, Willie?"

"Looks like it to me."

Ketchum's eyes glittered. "Maybe Belle made a mistake, hey, Willie? Grabbin' Joady. Didn't know the kind of critter he was. Mebbe if we sent her back, Diana might forgive and forget."

Joady glared. "Ketch, you are one lousy coyote. You jest can't stand that I got Belle and you got nothin'. It sticks in your throat. You keep tryin' to bust it. Well, you ain't. Only thing you're gonna bust is your gut if you keep yammerin' about it."

Willie glared at them. "I tole you before, Joady, that

bringin' a filly with us wasn't smart. It starts bad feelin's. I see it happenin'. Fact is, Joady, she's hurtin' the bunch. And the bunch ain't much any more. We three were the heart and soul of it. Looks like there's none left but us. Crazy to fight like this. Don't want any more of it."

He stoked the fire and they watched him silently. "We made a good haul at Tucson, got enough money to live fat on the hog for a time." His cold gray eyes studied Belle. "She's a beautiful young filly, and I can understand your feelin' for her, Joady, but she's crackin' things between us. Might be smart to send her back to Diana. We might just get rid of them cussed hungry wolves trackin' us."

The moon, big and silver, was climbing, but nobody was looking.

Joady's face set like granite. He looked at Belle. "She may not be much, but she's what I want just now. So, if she goes, I go."

Willie stared gimlet-eyed at Joady. "I learned a few things in my life, and one is that a mule-headed man dies an early death."

Joady grinned slowly. "Nobody gets a bullet in me. Ain't happened yet, and won't."

Willie grunted. "Lotta men pushing daises once thought like that."

They were silent, looking into the fire. Ketchum glanced at Belle, who was biting her lip. Suddenly they all looked at her.

She spoke softly. "Willie, I don't like you decidin' about me. Don't I have anything to say?"

Willie grinned. "Guess not, little filly. You took up

with bad hombres and you're gonna have to play our way."

She turned. "And you, Joady, been mighty insultin' to a lady you're s'posed to be fond of."

Joady laughed, bit on a chaw of tobacco. "Tell you the truth, Belle, I ain't been much for being fond of the ladies. When I got born it killed my ma. And Dad never forgave me for that. Whaled the tar outa me for nothin', on account of blamin' me for her dyin'."

Willie spoke sharply. "He was rotten with whiskey before you came into the world, Joady."

They were silent again. Belle gazed at the big moon rising slowly, touching the towers of granite with an edge of silver, throwing deep black shadows behind the soaring peaks. Again she wondered what she had got into. She'd been caught by passion and landed in the middle of a bunch of robbers. Though she still felt pleasure in Joady's arms, she realized he was a goat in his feelings for her. She wondered what lay ahead. Though Willie talked softly, it was what *he* said that counted. She stole a glance at Ketchum. He'd been watching her, and he sent her a small smile: she felt comforted. Ketchum was gentle and offered protection. It was a shame that she had hitched up with Joady, who had a touch of brutality.

Joady, suddenly alert to Ketchum's glance, glared jealously at him. "What the hell's in your mind, you polecat?"

Ketchum's eyes narrowed. "I'm thinkin' how bad you treat this li'l honey. You jest don't know how to take care of something real nice. You're like a lean, mean coyote skulking around spoilin' everything he touches.

That's what's in my mind."

Joady gaped, then flung himself at Ketch, trying to grab his throat. Ketch slipped out of those big hands and came up with a knee into Joady's gut. Joady paled, then swung for Ketchum's ribs. Ketchum tried to dance back, but part of the punch landed and it jolted him. He swung for Joady's jaw, and there was the crack of fist against bone. Joady staggered, shook his head, and came flailing his fists. Ketchum pulled back and they stood still, fists clenched, breathing hard, looking for an opening.

Willie, standing hard-faced, had been watching, part of him enjoying the fight, part worried. He could live with fists; it was guns that worried him.

Then an arrow whistled through the air and hit Ketchum's left shoulder. Willie twisted and fired in the direction of a giant boulder high to the right, and threw himself to the ground. Joady, too, though dazed from the fighting, also pulled his gun and crouched, but could see nothing to fire at. Ketchum pulled Belle down and watched Willie and Joady crawl forward and fan out in a move to circle the boulder. Belle, watching, heard the muted sound of hoofbeats. Willie, who had been crouching, ran forward. The bronze-bodied Apache was flailing the flanks of his pony with his legs.

Willie took careful aim and fired. He waited with bated breath, saw the Apache jerk. He'd been hit, Willie was sure, but just kept riding. Damned Apache—why did he get into the fight? Probably thought it a good time to pick off the palefaces, Willie thought.

He came back to Ketchum, sitting against the boulder. Belle, using Ketchum's knife, had cut the shirt around the arrow. The arrowhead was half-buried in the flesh of his left shoulder. Four inches lower and it would have hit his heart.

Willie grunted, took the knife from her, and held it to the fire. Joady came over, looked at Belle sitting close to Ketchum, and his jaw hardened. He said nothing.

"Give him whiskey, Belle," Willie said. Ketchum took a long pull. He drew breath, and Willie waited until he took another.

Willie turned to Joady. "See how loco it is for you two to rip at each other? There's plenty of 'em out there ready to do it."

He bent down and deftly cut the flesh around the arrowhead. Blood oozed out. Then he cut again and gently pulled the head out of the flesh. He blotted the blood with cloths which Joady brought from his saddle. He washed the wound with whiskey, and strapped cloths against the flesh.

Belle watched calmly. The blood didn't bother her.

Willie growled. "You're a gutsy filly." He looked at Joady and at Ketchum. "Got enough of fightin', you two?"

Ketchum shrugged and Joady looked away.

Willie gritted his teeth. Bring a woman into a bunch, it goes bad, he thought.

He'd have to do something about Belle.

The sun was climbing in a clear washed sky when Slocum saw the Apache bent dead over his pony. It was extraordinary the way the pony drifted along as if headed for some sacred hunting ground.

The Apache, realizing his time was up, had tied himself to the pony and it seemed as if he had given it a secret command before he died.

Slocum and Diana, on their horses, watched the Apache go past. He was bronze, well-built, with a red band around his long hair. The dried blood of the wound in his back told Slocum what had happened.

"I reckon Willie's bunch did it," Slocum said. "Just wonder what damage the Apache did."

Diana's brown eyes gleamed fiercely. "I hope Willie's still around for my gun. And I hate it that Belle's with those polecats."

"It's not good, and the quicker we get to her the better."

"Will we ever catch up, Slocum?" Her tone had a touch of despair.

"We'll get to him somewhere." Slocum pulled out a havana and lit it with a lucifer. "Odd that he hasn't stopped to tackle us. I suppose it has to do with you being Belle's sister. He'd like to pump me full of lead, but he draws the line with you."

Diana's lip curled with contempt. "He's scared to face me. Been running all the time."

Slocum couldn't help smiling. "Scared? I find it hard to believe the famous robber Willie James is scared of a woman." Then he scratched his head. "Maybe he remembers how you shoot."

"Maybe he remembers more than that," she said sullenly. "How I'd like to get him in my sights."

There it was again, the powerful hate she had for Willie James. Something queer about it, and Slocum sure wished he could put a handle on it. She was ferocious about Willie, and he wondered if it had more to do with the gang stealing Belle or the money. Whatever it was, he had his own grievance, and that was why he was tracking these stinking hyenas. They were thieves, killers, had tried to hang him, stolen money, stolen an innocent girl. Any of these tricks called for lynching.

He rubbed his chin thoughtfully and looked at the trail the bunch had taken. It curved around a big hill rise and twisted on toward Tombstone. Slocum studied the hill and wondered if it had a crossing, once you got past the thick brush, maybe some narrow old Indian trail used by Apaches for bypassing the hill.

Diana looked irritable. "Why are we waiting, Slocum? We're losing time."

"I'm thinking there might be a shortcut. A trail over this hill used by the Indians long ago."

She looked up, frowning, seeing nothing. "And it might be a wild-goose chase. Then we'll have to retrace our ground."

"Worth a try, if you hope to catch them. They're too far ahead."

She stared up glumly, feeling it was a long shot.

"Let's do it," Slocum said firmly. He sensed something about the slope, the way the brush grew.

"All right," she said. "You haven't lost a trail yet. Must know what you're doing."

They started to climb, and the going, at the beginning, was rough, straining the horses. They had to stop a few times, but as they moved into the thick brush, they found it, a narrow old Apache trail.

The sun was high when they approached a clearing. Slocum rode through it and to his amazement saw Willie's bunch not more than a hundred yards away. They were passing a pocket of boulders, and Willie, riding in front, his body alert, his eyes scanning, instantly picked up Slocum. It jolted him, and he yelled to alert the others, pulled at the reins of his horse, heading it toward the boulders, and jerked his gun. Slocum, too, went for his gun, but it was pointless to shoot, though both of them did. They were out of range for pistols.

Slocum jumped from his horse, grabbed his rifle out of its saddle holster, and fired, his bullet chipping the boulder inches over Joady's head. They, too, fired rifles, forcing Slocum to hit the ground, and by the time he was able to raise his head they had moved into the pocket of boulders, and were safe behind them.

Slocum cursed softly. He should have been prepared. He turned to look at Diana. Her eyes were glowing with excitement. "By God, you almost nailed Joady! And Belle was with them, did you see?"

"Yeah, and I had a shot at Joady and missed."

She looked down at the pocket of boulders that lay astride the trail; the four of them were lurking there, about one hundred yards away.

"We got 'em, Slocum," she exulted. "We got high position. They move, we nail them, right?"

He studied the layout and slowly nodded. "We've got good position, but they can move back, staying behind those boulders. And after dark, they can ride."

She glanced at the sky. "Five hours before dark. They won't stay put. Willie is an impatient man."

"Reckon so," he muttered, his piercing green eyes studying the surrounding land. "The bunch can always make a run for it, if they shoot as they ride. It's hard to shoot straight if you're ducking bullets."

Would they think of it? he wondered. They might,

after a time. Just now it looked like a standoff. Once the dark came down the bunch could try a getaway. He didn't himself like this setup. He chewed his lip, frustrated.

She'd been watching him. "What now, Slocum?"

"It's not the way I hoped to trap 'em, Diana," he drawled, holding his rifle ready. "In a way, it's a standoff."

Her lovely face went into a deep scowl. "What do you mean, standoff? They can't move."

"We can't either." He peered from behind the big boulder that shielded both of them. "Let's hope someone gets a bit careless."

And that, in fact, seemed almost to happen as Joady peered out for a fraction of a second, pulling back instantly. Slocum's bullet splintered the stone where Joady's face had been.

Slocum smiled. "Let him know we're here."

In malicious response, two bullets hit both ends of the boulder behind which they crouched, splintering rock. Joady and Willie had both fired at one time.

"Reckon they're letting us know they're here, too," Slocum said grimly.

She sat on a small rock, holding her rifle, and chafed. She pulled off her small Stetson and the sun lit her dark brown hair.

"Can you figure out something?" she asked.

"When it's darker, I might try to get down and circle them. If they don't move before that. But you'd be here alone."

"If you attack from behind, it might force them forward. I'll be waitin'." Her face was hard.

He pulled out a havana and lit it. "There's nothing to

do for a time," he said. "That sun has to move. 'Cause they ain't movin'. And we can't." He gazed at her beautiful face. It always astonished him, how bloodthirsty she was about Willie James. You wouldn't expect a woman so lovely to sound so poisonous.

"Tell me Diana. How'd you make the mistake of hiring a man like Willie James?"

She turned away, as if he had touched a sore point. She looked at the distant Catalinas, then spoke slowly. "When I make a mistake, it's a big one. Yet, at the time, it didn't seem like one. I told you before. When Dad died I needed a strong man to take over the ranch. Willie James was in town, and it seems he heard a few things about the money in our ranch. It seemed to have caught his interest. He put himself in my way. He was good-looking, strong. It was easy to go wrong. It all broke up when Joady got drunk and grabbed Belle."

He stared at her, which made her uncomfortable. She seemed to be holding something back, and didn't seem crazy about the way the conversation was going. She tried to shift it.

"What about you, Slocum? Don't know much about you." She smiled. "You look like a man who's done a lot in his life. Where'd you start from?"

He peered past the boulder; all was quiet. "I'm a Georgia man."

She smiled. "Doesn't take much to know that, Slocum. That drawl of yours. So what happened? We seem to have time before dark. You could tell me the story of your life."

He laughed. "There isn't that much time."

"All right. So how'd you lose the ole plantation?"

She was astonished at the way his face hardened and his eyes gleamed.

"We had a war, you may remember. After some gory fighting and a spell with Quantrill in Kansas, I went back to Calhoun County and found a lowdown critter claiming my land. Our family's land, going back generations. Carpetbagger. I tried to reason with him. He insisted, so I had to use force." He shrugged. "Made me a travelling man." He flipped his cigar, watched it tumble in the air. "After a time, I came out to the Territory, where a man can start fresh and make a life. I seen it happen. Trouble is that not only the settlers came out but a lotta scum crawled outa the holes of the East, gangs, livin' off decent folk. To tell the truth, nothing I hate more than a thieving rat who'll kill for money."

Diana listened, occasionally glancing to the boulders below. Now she looked hard at Slocum's face. It was strong, bronzed, lean, with piercing green eyes, high cheekbones. A handsome man, she thought, and felt his magnetism. She saw his face harden.

"I particularly want," he said, "to take good care of the polecats down there. They strung me up for no reason, ready to kill. I got a particular hate for that." He glanced at her. "And I have a particularly tender feeling about you and your shooting eye."

The smile on her face widened. "So you have tender feelin's for me, do you, Slocum?"

He grinned. "Very tender."

"Don't do much to express your feelings, do you?"

That jolted him. He looked into her beautiful face, the soft inviting brown eyes, the red curving lips, the swell of her breasts.

He cursed under his breath. If ever a woman was ready for a bit of loving, this one was. And he, too, felt a surge of animal excitement. He looked again at her breasts, and felt the lust come strong on him. He threw a glance down on the trail. Three killers crouched there, and the dumbest thing in the world would be to make a move at Diana at a time like this. What he needed was to concentrate on them, not on this beautiful filly whose appeal could bring them to sudden ruin.

Her lips were parted, and she looked at him, and the appeal was so strong that he leaned forward and she put her lips up for kissing. Maybe he could just kiss and hold her, keeping an eye on what was happening down on the trail.

He would try.

Again he pressed his lips to hers, and was astonished at the way she responded, her mouth open, hungry for love. His body stiffened with longing, and his hand went over her breast. Her breasts were full, womanly, shapely; he slipped his hand under her shirt, felt the soft skin, the erect nipple. He brought his body against hers, his swollen flesh against her loins.

She sighed, and her body went limp.

They were behind the huge boulder, and again he wondered if this was madness. They could lose their quarry. At any moment Willie's bunch could start to ride, shooting fast to keep the two of them under cover. Slocum, kissing her, had to stop and look out. No movement; oh, yes, just a face peering out, wondering about the silence. That was a stroke of luck. He grabbed his rifle and fired at the corner of the boulder, splintering stone.

He grinned. Diana was still sunk in her passions, bewildered by his action.

"That should give us a bit of time," he said. "This game, Diana, is gonna have to be fast or nothing at all. Which will it be?"

Her eyes glowed and he could tell it was a dumb question. He opened her shirt, brought out her breasts, big, beautiful, and pink-nippled, and put his tongue to one. She sighed.

"This has to be fast," he muttered, and opened the buttons of her Levi's, pulled at them, to start her. Then he pulled off his own Levi's. Standing nude, she was marvelous to look at; the billowing hips, slender waist, the curly hair shyly covering the pink lips between her thighs. He felt a powerful rush of excitement, and couldn't help grinning; the threat of death from below in the boulders seemed to increase the excitement of the sex.

Again he tongued her breasts, and his hands went over her waist and rounded buttocks, then his hand went between her thighs, his finger probing the lush, wet warmth. She moaned softly. He peered one last time from behind the boulder, saw no movement, brought her gently to the ground. Her thighs went apart, and his swollen organ slipped in. She was tight, marvelously tight, but wet and wonderful, and he went in slowly, entirely filling her. She groaned softly.

Well, he thought, this is making love under the gun, it can't be a long-time thing. He began to move hard, holding her hips, and her body responded; his hands moved over her breasts, her buttocks..He kissed her, and her lips clung to him. Again his body began to move;

he began to pump hard, in and out, and each thrust made her whine, as if she felt a mix of pain and pleasure. As his passion zoomed, his thrusts came quicker and fiercer, then the sensations started, the wild, crazy surging. He grunted at the pleasure, and he could tell her body was going into its spasm of pleasure. She grabbed him, held his body in a grip.

They lay together like this, then he became aware of movement below. He swore under his breath. This had been crazy. Something was about to happen.

He pulled away from her. She looked just out of it, could have died happy at the moment, he thought, as he grabbed his rifle and peered out.

Someone!

He brought up his rifle, then lowered it.

Belle was coming toward them, her hand held up.

He turned to Diana. "It's Belle," he said, and slipped on his Levi's. She moved, too, as if in a trance, as she slipped into her Levi's, buttoned her shirt.

"Don't get shot, Slocum," she whispered to him. "If this is quick, I want the slow version."

He laughed.

Then her face hardened as, peering past the boulder, she saw Belle standing twenty yards away.

# 10

Nothing shocked Willie James more, while he was leading his bunch on the trail to Tombstone, than the sudden sight of Slocum and Diana up on a rocky hill that he had judged uncrossable.

He stayed cool, however, and yelled sharply at the others, firing at Slocum though he was out of range. He spurred his horse sharply to the left into a pocket of boulders; the others followed.

He swung off the saddle with his rifle, as did Joady, and they peered out. Slocum and Diana had disappeared behind a huge boulder that faced down on the trail.

Willie cursed softly under his breath, aware that Slocum had the firing position. He glanced about, and realized there was no way the bunch could break out of this pocket safely. Diana was a sharpshooter and he had to believe Slocum was no slouch either.

On the other hand, Slocum's position wasn't all that

good; he couldn't stick his head out. It was a standoff. Joady stuck his head out to look, and a rifle bullet bounced off the edge of the boulder.

Joady swore and fired, as did Willie, their bullets hitting each end of the boulder behind which Slocum crouched. They smiled at each other.

"Let 'em know they can't move either," Willie grumbled. He pulled a cigarillo and lit it, still crouched.

"Don't none of you, for the time being, put your heads out," he said. "We know Diana's a deadeye."

Joady looked sullen. "What do you aim to do, Willie? Not goin' to stay here."

"Where would you like to go, Joady?" Willie said calmly.

Joady's dark face scowled. "We gotta make a move. There's only two of 'em."

"There's only three of us. And I'm not sure that Ketchum can be much help."

"My shootin' arm's good, Willie," Ketchum said quietly.

"They got the position," Willie said, scanning the land. "We may have to wait till dark."

"Dark!" Joady growled. "I ain't gonna crouch here four hours."

"What else would you do?"

"We make a run for it, shootin' at them."

"They'll be standing, shootin' straight, and we'll be shootin' from running horses. Who d'ye think is gonna get hit, mulehead?"

"Don't call me mulehead, Willie."

"I'd rather not, 'cept you talk like one. Now we'll mull it over, mebbe come up with something."

"How'd they get up there?" asked Belle. "Get so close. I thought they were five hours behind us."

"They were," said Willie. "That Slocum has a smart head. He figgered a trail over the mountain. I never figgered on one. He cut four hours of travelling time."

"So what do we do about this polecat, Slocum?" Joady asked fretfully. "I'm sick of runnin'."

Willie grinned. "You're a man of short patience, Joady. Never reasoned out anything. Lemme consider it."

He smoked and thought. They were carrying a hell of a lot of money, not only the money he'd grabbed from Diana, but the bank money. He didn't intend to lose it by taking foolish risks. That damned Slocum was one hell of a trailsman.

Willie glanced at Belle. Maybe she was the answer. She was sweet on Joady—Ketch, too, for that matter. He himself found the little filly interesting. He had been ready, at one time, to send her back to Diana just to ease the tension in the bunch. Ketch and Joady fighting over her was bad. He could send her back, but should he? Joady might get mean, but he'd seen Joady go through fits like these over a filly before, and come out all right.

"Belle."

She looked at Willie.

"Do you like it, being with us?"

She smiled. "Like it? Why, yes, Willie."

"How'd you like to help us?"

Joady and Ketch were listening sharply.

"Do what, Willie?" she asked.

"You mosey up that hill. Not hard. Stop 'bout twenty yards in front of them and give 'em a message."

"What message?"

"Tell 'em to move back. We want a couple of hours headway."

She stared at him. "Why would they do that, Willie?"

His face widened in a malicious grin. "Tell 'em that if they don't, we're gonna shoot your tail off, right in front of them."

There was a long moment of silence.

She looked into his gray eyes. They were stony, icy, and she knew suddenly he wasn't fooling. She looked at Joady. His lips were tight, but he said nothing. Ketch, too, looked taut.

"What if they don't believe it?"

Willie stroked his cheek. "Then we'll have to prove it, won't we?" He turned to look at the men. Joady's lips were tight.

Ketch said, "I don't like it, Willie."

Willie's voice went silky. "It'll never come to it, Ketch. They won't take the chance. They'll move back."

"Then what?" Ketch asked.

"Then we run."

"What about Belle?"

Willie smiled. "What would you want to happen, Ketch?"

"She comes back with us," he said.

"Sure," said Willie. "There's one thing."

The men watched him.

"You muleheads are not gonna dogfight over her, are you? 'Cause if you do, she doesn't come back."

Belle stared at him. "What's that mean, Willie? You shoot me."

"Listen, honey, we got some big money here, and I'm gonna do my best to protect it."

"You and your damned money," Belle muttered.

"What's that, Belle?" Willie's eyes flashed ice. Then he grinned. "Lemme tell you. You been amusin' my brother, Joady, and that's fine. But we have gone through a lotta fillies in our time, and to my way o' thinkin' you're just another. If you do anything that ain't jest right up there, cute filly or not, you're gonna get blasted." His voice had taken a chilling tone. "Jest so you understand." He stared coldly at Joady and Ketchum. His jaw was hard, and his gray eyes burned steadily at them.

Belle couldn't help shivering. She'd suddenly seen the Willie James the Territory knew about, a cold, ruthless killer who didn't care who he killed, if they were in the way.

Belle climbed the hill slowly, aware that every so often someone down below was glancing out to watch her. She did as she'd been told, stopped twenty yards short of the big boulder that shielded Diana and Slocum.

They knew she was there because she heard Diana. "Good God, Belle, don't stand there, keep comin'."

"They won't let me, Diana."

"What d'ye mean, honey?"

"Willie wants me to give you a message," Belle said. Slocum's eyes narrowed and he gripped his rifle.

"Message, Belle?" repeated Diana. "Well, come in here and tell it."

"I can't go any further. They tole me to stop here. I can't come up."

Diana cursed softly. "What are you s'posed to tell us?"

"Willie wants you to move back. Give him 'bout a coupla hours headway."

Slocum's jaw clenched.

"And what if we don't?" Diana said.

"They'll shoot me." Belle's voice was flat.

There was a silence, then Slocum cursed. Diana's eyes flashed fear. She looked at Slocum. "Do you think they mean it?"

His teeth were grinding. "Yeah, I think so."

Diana's eyes glinted with rage. "He's the most rotten dog that ever drew breath."

Belle waited silently. Then she said, "Guess you got my life in your hands."

Diana kicked the dirt at her feet. "Can't believe that mangy polecat would come up with something like this."

"He's got a lot of money, Diana. He's killed before to get it. He'll kill again to keep it," Slocum said.

"So what do we do?"

"We'll do it. And hope to catch up in Tombstone."

Diana grimaced. "Damnit. Hate to give up a position like this. We got them in a corner."

He smiled. "We can't let them shoot Belle."

"Don't believe they will," she said suddenly. "Shoot a woman, a young girl."

"Guess you don't know who you're dealing with," Slocum said. "He's a killer. I think he'll do it."

Diana squirmed, leaned against the boulder, bowed her head in frustrated anger. "Why'd you go with them, Belle?" she demanded. "How could you be so dumb?"

"I'm sorry, Diana. Jest didn't think all this would happen. How could I know the man you married would turn out to be Willie James?"

Slocum scowled. He turned the remark over in his head. Diana married to Willie? It sounded crazy. So that was why Diana had all this hate. She'd been deceived. Willie had married her to get cover, to go underground till the heat of the trailing posse had cooled down.

So Diana had married him, probably had strong feelings about him, but when it suited him, Willie just grabbed her money and ran. No wonder she wanted to shoot his butt off.

Diana was looking at him, her lips tight. "Slocum, I been meanin' to tell you, again and again, but couldn't. It was crazy. He was a good-looking, strong cowboy, he threw a spell on me. Who'd of thought he'd be Willie James."

He shrugged. The famous woman's intuition didn't seem to be working.

A pistol shot was fired into the air.

Belle jumped. "For pity's sake, Diana, say something."

Slocum stared at the sky, a sheet of brass. Far in the distance a big lone bird swung its wings in slow motion as it looked over the land for a meal.

"Let her go," Slocum said, hard-eyed.

"All right. Go back to them," Diana said. "Tell 'em they've got the time, that we'll move back. And for God's sake, Belle, get hold of a gun and kill Willie."

Belle just stared at her. "Goodbye, Diana." She turned to go, but stopped. "Willie also said if you tried to trick him, he'd still have me. That you better think of me as a hostage."

Diana gritted her teeth. She'd been hoping to sneak a shot at Willie, get him when he started to ride, but he seemed to have figured that out. She slouched, a bit disheartened, and they walked to their horses.

She was about to put her foot into the stirrup, then said, "Should we go back, Slocum? Why keep our word to scum like them?"

Slocum lit a havana, flipped the lucifer into the air.

"How d'ye suppose they'll ride out? Willie will have Belle sitting in front of him, a gun on her. Joady will be pulling her horse." He shook his head. "Willie may be a lot of rotten things, but dumb he ain't."

Her teeth clenched. "God, how I hate that man."

They rode back slowly over the narrow trail pitted with small rocks and short brush, then dismounted. Not long after, Slocum's keen ears picked up the faraway neigh of a horse.

It was a shame, Slocum thought; they had had him bottled up, but Willie had outfoxed them. That was how it was when you had to fight against an outlaw who kicked at the rules, who would do anything to protect himself.

They sat in the shade of a nearby boulder and Slocum pulled out his canteen. It was a broiler of a day, and he poured water into his hat and gave some to the horses. He rubbed the flanks of his roan, looked into the liquid black eyes of the horse, and it seemed to him he saw love. Slocum felt a strong stir of feeling: his best friend.

He glanced at Diana. Her beautiful face was taut. "I'spose you think me a fool for marrying up with a man like Willie."

He shrugged. "You didn't know he was a famous outlaw."

She shook her head in self-disgust. "Guess I was too hard hit 'bout the death of Dad. I needed to lean on a strong man. And Willie was smart and strong; he had appealing ways. 'Cause I needed a man, he just seemed to fit. How'd I know he had found out a lot of things about me before he put himself in my way? But I see now he didn't give a fig about me. When he decided to run, he just took off with my money. Like that. A man with no love, just greed." She gazed at Slocum with tight lips. "You'd say he took grievous advantage of me, right, Slocum?"

He looked at her somberly. "Yeah, I'd say that."

"So you can understand why I have this great hate. Why I want most to get him in my sights."

Slocum grinned. "Willie is slick. He is not the man to put himself in your sights. He might just aim to put you in *his* sights."

She shrugged. "I'll take my chances." Then she looked at him archly. "And I got you, Slocum."

He smiled. "You got me." He looked at her curving, sensual body, thinking that he'd like to have it, but the moment didn't seem right. He glanced at the sky. The sun looked like a blistered yellow disk, and had started to slide down.

He moved to the roan, swung over the saddle. "Let's go to Tombstone and nail those thieving rats to the wall."

It was just getting dark when Willie walked his horse into Tombstone at the head of the bunch. The lamps in the buildings poured light into the street; it was a festive time when cowboys, saddle-sore from riding the range in the hot sun, were now in for fun. And the place they came for fun was Saunders's Saloon, abundant with whiskey, women, and anything that promised action.

Willie listened to the rambunctious sounds, and

grinned. It was his kind of town, it was badland territory, and the desperado made it his favorite watering hole. Once in a while a stout-hearted lawman drifted into town in pursuit of an outlaw, but most lawmen stayed clear of Tombstone.

A great town, Willie told himself. As he walked toward the saloon, he looked at the motley gang—pink-cheeked cowboys, hard-bitten range men, hatchet-faced thieves, old-timers, the lot.

He thought of Slocum. He thought about Slocum a great deal, felt that Slocum deserved the most careful attention. Willie had hunches, and he had learned to listen to them. His hunch told him that Slocum was a deadly hunter of men, and that he should be treated with great care if you didn't want to end up pushing daisies in boot hill.

Willie was thinking hard about Slocum. This polecat had, it seemed, single-handedly knocked off the remnant of the gang, men Willie expected to join him: Biggers, Snouts, Mike, Burt, Tom. Tough men, good with guns. Where were they? Was it a fluke? Where in hell were Burt and his boys? No way of knowing. But why give credit to Slocum? Could he be exaggerating Slocum's gunplay? Joady didn't think Slocum was such a hot gun. But Joady's judgment couldn't be trusted. So what was to be done? Something smart. Before this night was over, Slocum and Diana would be in Tombstone. He had to have something ready.

Well, he had Belle. She gave him the edge. Look how easy he had slipped out of that boulder bottleneck by using her. She was his ace.

He glanced back at Belle. She was riding alongside

of Ketchum in her pert brown hat, low-cut blouse that showed part of her breasts, a peaches and cream skin, a straight delicate nose with flashing blue eyes that glowed when they looked at men.

At the beginning, Willie didn't want her along, figuring it'd be mighty sticky. And he was right—look how Joady and Ketch got into a slugging match about that hussy. Now, he felt different. He felt perked by the filly, not too fond, because long ago, he'd learned a woman could put you under the hammer. Now he had an itch for her. She was fresh as a peach, not like the frowsy whores you saw in the saloons. He thought of her lithe young body, her cute butt, her well-packed bust. She was a choice hunk of female, and he ought to make time for her. And Joady? Would he throw a fit? Naw. Joady always went hard at first for a filly, but then he tired of them. No, Willie didn't think he'd run into any trouble with Joady.

He dismounted in front of the saloon, tied the reins to the railpost, watched Belle swing gracefully off her horse. "Let's get a couple of drinks," he said cheerfully. She'd go in with them, and any dumb cowpoke who dared make a remark would get his ears pinned back.

He swung through the batwing doors, followed by the others.

It was a big, smoky saloon, with a bunch of men hanging on the round bar, hard-bitten, lean-faced men, some boisterous young cowboys, some old-timers. Skimpy-dressed whores floated around the tables where the men gambled. The barkeep, Saunders, a man with muttonchop whiskers, popped his eyes at the sight of Willie and quickly brought a couple of whiskey bottles and glasses to the table where Willie's bunch took their seats.

"Hi, Willie," Saunders said softly. "Nice to see ya." His shrewd blue eyes swept round at Joady, Ketch, and Belle, and he nodded politely.

"Saunders, you ole coyote," chuckled Willie, "you ain't changed a bit since the old days in Dodge City, the old muttonchop whiskers." He leaned forward and spoke in a low voice. "Lookin' for Burt and the boys. Seen anything of them?"

"Not hide nor hair. Only man here is Deadeye Dunay."

Willie's eyes gleamed. Deadeye! He was a real hot pistol. Good man to use. "Where's he at?"

"Where he's usually at," Saunders said, jerking his finger toward the rooms upstairs. "With the ladies."

Willie looked at Joady and Ketch. They all grinned. Deadeye Dunay was a great one for ladies of the evening.

"It'll be great to see Deadeye," Willie said as a plan began to form in his mind.

Joady poured whiskey into all the glasses. "Well, here we are in Tombstone. A great place to bury Slocum." He laughed harshly and gulped his drink.

"Yeah," said Willie, "let's drink to Tombstone. Slocum's last resting place." They all drank except Belle.

Willie stared at her. "Well, Belle?"

"Must I drink this stuff, Willie?"

In the silence, a tipsy saloon woman in a short red skirt and a silky blouse all bulky with breast stopped at their table.

"You don't hafta, honey, I'll drink it for yuh." She lifted the glass to her lips and emptied it, then smiled at all, and walked off, unsteady on her pins.

"She got ya drink, Belle," said Joady.

Belle laughed. "Thank the lady."

"Hasn't been a lady for thirty years, " Joady growled. He poured another. "You'll feel better with whiskey in you, honey."

"I feel all right now."

"Drink it," said Willie. "No time to be a goody girl."

"Why force it?" Ketch asked.

Joady and Willie stared at him. "What the hell's the matter, Ketch?"

"The kid doesn't care to drink. So let her be." He smiled at them. "We'll do enough drinkin' for her."

Willie nodded slowly, but looked gimlet-eyed at Ketch.

"He's got a big soft spot for Belle," Joady smirked, guzzling his drink.

"She's a good kid," Ketchum said.

"You bet," said Willie, and he looked at Belle. Her eyes flashed; she hated the way they talked about her as if she wasn't there, but they were desperadoes, and she shouldn't expect anything different. Well, she had always craved excitement in her life, but this was a bit more than she bargained for.

She noticed a hatchet-faced cowboy just sauntering past the table; he stopped to stare at her, his eyes sticking like glue. "Now, that's whut I call a fancy saloon pussy," he drawled. "Fresh as a peach and twice as good-lookin'." He turned to the men. "If you boys are through with the young hussy, how 'bout me taking a piece of her? Cutter's the name, Dan Cutter."

Ketchum's dark eyes narrowed. "Cutter, why don't you cut the hell outa here so you can stay healthy."

Cutter's leathery hatchet face went into a scowl.

"What's the matter with you, cowboy? I don't want to buy her, just rent her. She sho' looks like a hot young piece."

Ketchum came out of his chair like a shot and swung for Cutter's jaw. It jolted him, but he was rawboned and hard. He swung back at Ketch, hitting his cheek, ripping the flesh. Everyone in the bar stopped to watch. Ketch's left shoulder had been nicked by an arrow, but it didn't seem to slow him down. He swung hard with his right at Cutter's gut, and Cutter grunted. He stood square and swung a right that Ketch parried; he threw a hard right at Cutter's nose and it spouted blood. Cutter wiped the blood off his nose, swore violently, lowered his head to butt Ketch in the gut. Ketch took a nimble step sideways, swung his big fist at Cutter's jaw. Cutter looked stunned. His knees suddenly buckled and he went down to the floor, lay flat on his back, eyes closed.

The men in the saloon had been watching the fight with huge enjoyment, and when Cutter dropped, a roar of pleasure went up. The cowboys were high on whiskey, and nothing pleased them more than a thumping good fistfight.

A couple of men pulled the groggy Cutter to the side, where someone threw a glass of water at his face to revive him.

"Not bad for a one-armed man, Ketch," Willie said.

Joady shook his head. "You shoulda conked him with a bottle 'stead of wasting punches."

Ketch sat next to Belle. She smiled at him, untied his neckerchief, and tenderly wiped the blood off his cheek.

"Thank you, Ketch. You're a red-blooded man." She

glared at Joady. "I expected you to do somethin', not let that polecat insult me."

Joady yawned. "S'pose I might have, but Ketch was in a hurry to protect your honor. I woulda put a bullet up his tail, not soil my hands on him."

"Woulda and shoulda," Belle said. "But it's nothin' till a man does somethin'." And again she flashed Ketchum a big smile.

"You're a good kid, Belle," said Ketchum, and looked at Willie.

Willie's piercing gray eyes were staring at a man coming down from one of the upstairs rooms.

"Deadeye Dunay, best ladies' man in the Territory," said Willie.

Deadeye heard the voice, turned, grinned hugely, came to the table. He had a drooping mustache in a lean, dark face, and a scar at his mouth giving it a sinister twist when he smiled.

He stared appreciatively at Belle, but was smart enough to say nothing. He nodded at Joady and Ketchum. "Good to see yuh, Willie. Been expectin' yuh. How'd things go in Tucson?"

"They went good," Willie said. "You shoulda been there."

"I'd'a been there if I could, Willie. I had McCarthy, an ornery lawman, stickin' on my tail, and it took some doin' to get rid of him."

"Wouldn't expect you to have trouble, Deadeye," said Joady.

Deadeye shrugged. "He was a stubborn cuss. I picked him off three miles short of Tombstone." He sat down, poured a whiskey. "Who's the pretty lady?"

"Belle's the name," said Willie, his voice edged. "She's with us."

Deadeye's sinister smile twisted his face. He had just learned from the tone in Willie's voice that Belle was off limits. He looked at Joady and Ketchum. "Where's the others? Expectin' to see Burt and the boys."

After a silence, Willie said grimly, "A polecat name of Slocum got in their way."

Deadeye stared. "Whut d'ye mean?" He rubbed his nose vigorously, which he sometimes did when jarred. "You ain't tellin' me that this one polecat called Slocum knocked out the boys?"

"Mebbe yes, mebbe no. Don't know for sure about Burt and the boys. They never got to where they were s'posed to be. Slocum did take Snouts and Biggers."

"Did he? Damn his hide." He looked thoughtful. "Poor Biggers, I was lookin' forward to seein' him." Then he shook his head. "But they were sticky-fingered when it came to pullin' guns, those two." Deadeye looked questioningly at Joady.

Joady shrugged. "I tole Willie, I'd take Slocum out by myself. But he set up a squawk."

"That polecat is fast," said Willie, "no point denying it. Why risk a mess when we can do it clean? Why a shootout when, instead, we jest put a bullet in his back? Do it easy."

Deadeye looked at Belle, as if embarrassed. "Never cared about that kinda thing, Willie. Rubs me the wrong way. I'll be glad to take this Slocum straight on. Insult him, force him to draw."

"Do it if you want, Deadeye. But you gotta have backup."

"He shot Biggers, a mighty good friend. Don't like the idea of this polecat walking around after he shot Biggers. I'll take this Slocum straight on."

Willie stared. 'I'm tellin' you, he's fast."

Deadeye smiled grimly. "It's when you cut down the fast gun that you build a rep in the Territory."

Willie studied him with a peculiar smile. "You got more guts than brains, Deadeye, but I can't help admiring you. Slocum's trailin' us. And we want to get rid of him. When Slocum comes, you can meet him head on. He won't figger you one of the bunch."

"I'll blast hell out of him for you, Willie. No need to worry."

Willie looked irritated. "I tole you, this polecat is fast."

Deadeye smiled. "That's good. No fun pullin' against a slow gun. No pride in that."

"You some kind of a mulehead?" Willie demanded. "The idea is for him to be dead, not for you to prove you're a great gunfighter."

"What the hell, Willie. Life's a crap shoot. You never know when you're gonna be mowed down. Live it short and sweet. I'll take on this Slocum polecat, and put him in the daisies."

Willie nodded thoughtfully. He had made a point of picking men like Deadeye. Fast-shooting, reckless, with iron in their guts. Such men were the backbone of the old bunch, but most of them had made the trip to boot hill. The good ones went first, Willie had found; all guts and dumb pride. Not his style. Smart men didn't take chances; they played the odds so that, when the sun came up the next day, they were still around to enjoy it. He'd let Deadeye believe he was going against Slocum, but arrange a secret backup. He wouldn't use Joady or Ketchum, but pick up an outlaw, put him on the roof with a rifle. That simple. Why argue with Deadeye?

"All right, Deadeye. Slocum's a big man, comin' in on a roan, with Diana, a good-looking woman. Won't be any trouble pickin' him up. You jest be waitin'." His grin was suddenly diabolical. "It'll all come out all right. In a coupla hours, Slocum will be dead in Tombstone."

# 11

From the rise of the hill, Slocum looked down at Tombstone. Oil lamps from the houses threw plenty of light
into the street, and festive sounds floated out to him. A
lively town with a deadly name: Tombstone. It had the
legends already, famous Boot Hill where famous gunfighters found their final rest. He thought of that corral
where three stout-hearted brothers stood side by side,
fighting for revenge to the bitter end. What future did
Tombstone have for him? he wondered. For Willie James?
Would the bunch hole up here and make their stand?
They were three, maybe more. Doubly dangerous going
into Tombstone, but more reason to face it, once for all,
get it done.

Slocum pulled out a havana and lit it, looking thoughtfully at the town lights. You had to work smart against
Willie. You didn't barge into a town like this; you could

barge right into a bullet. You felt your way in. Willie
wasn't the kind of a man who would stand out there and
invite a showdown. He was a thief, a killer, and a clever
coyote. Look at how he used Belle, promised to shoot
her if he was crossed, a mangy skunk. So how did you
fight him? He fought sly, never fought honest. Slyness
had brought him a long way.

Slocum looked at the sky, a great stretch of blue with
a round silver moon. How did you fight slyness? He
would drift into town, but not straight on; he would scout
it.

He rode back to where he'd left Diana, a sequestered
spot between trees and boulders. He swung off the roan
and looked up again at the millions of stars flung end-
lessly across the heavens.

The beauty of the night touched him. The world was
beautiful and it was good to be alive. But the town was
Tombstone and, lively as it was, it had the smell of death.
A vague foreboding swept through him. He didn't like
the feeling.

He walked toward Diana. She sat with her back against
a smooth boulder, the light of the moon glowing on her
brown hair, her creamy skin, the curve of her breast. A
strong sensual feeling streaked through him. He felt on
the edge of a showdown in Tombstone. But here was
Diana.

She was drinking coffee and when he looked at her,
she smiled. "What d'ye think, Slocum? Should we go
in now or in the mornin'?"

"Not in the morning. Willie'd have too good a look
at the target." He picked up the coffee pot and poured a
cupful. "I figure he's gonna try and spring a trap. We

just don't ride in. We drift in behind the houses and look. See what's what. Maybe nothing, maybe he's got Joady setting in the shadows against a wall, Ketch on the other side. Yes, Willie might be waiting. There's also a chance he picked up provisions and kept riding. No telling." He chewed his lip. "Meanwhile."

She waited for him to finish, but he didn't, just gazed at her, his eyes glowing. She looked up in surprise.

He cleared his throat. "I figure there's no hurry. We could relax a bit."

She sensed something in his tone and looked at him sharply. Then she smiled, a radiant smile.

"I have been wondering when it would hit you, Slocum. As an eager lover, you ain't the world's best."

He laughed. "Hard to be eager when you're aching for revenge, and tight on the trail of skunks."

He reached for her and she put her full red lips up for kissing. She rose to her feet, pressed her body hard against him. He could feel her full breasts against his chest. His hand slipped into her shirt. The soft velvet skin pleased him. He unbuttoned her shirt.

Her hand went down between his legs and she shamelessly unbuttoned his Levi's. His organ came out, lusty and fierce.

"You're every inch a man, Slocum," she said softly. She stroked his flesh, made soft sounds in her throat.

"Let's get outa these things, honey," he said, and started to peel.

The last time they had made love he had been in a rush, and maybe he had shortchanged her. He should try to do better.

When she stood in front of him he couldn't help but

whistle. Though he'd seen her body before, in the soft gleam of moonlight she looked like the statue of Diana he'd once seen in a magazine. Full hips, full breasts, slender waist, curving graceful thighs and legs, and that secret crease between her legs, covered shyly with curly brown hair.

"You're one good-lookin' woman, Diana," he muttered. And she, looking at his broad shoulders, lean hips, hefty chest, strong legs, and the powerful potency between them, couldn't help but think he was all male and all excitement.

He reached for her body, caressed her nipples, ran his hand over the rounded breasts, down along her waist, her hips, then put his fingers between her legs. Warm and wet. He lay her back and slipped over the silky flesh. His tongue worked over her breasts, until finally he slipped down and put his face between her thighs. His intense moves sent her into an ecstasy of sighs. She grabbed his head and made sounds deep in her throat. After a time, he pulled away and turned his body. She took hold of his ponderous excitement, her mouth opening for him. He felt enormous pleasure as her lips, tongue, and mouth moved with clever skill. He shut his eyes, delighting in his sensations. After a time, he pulled out, turned her, looked at the rounded shape of her buttocks, slipped between her thighs, and felt the snug warmth. Now he pushed deep, deeper; she squirmed with pleasure. He held her buttocks, thrusting in and out. He leaned over to hold her dangling breasts. Again and again he thrust, feeling her tight smooth warmth. Finally he turned her and her legs came apart to receive him, and again he went in, feeling huge excitement. He grasped her silky buttocks and began to drive. Her hips arched as she received his movements. He kept thrusting hard, and felt her body tighten with anguish and hold. Then she flung her arms around him, came up to meet his massive thrusting. He felt the sudden explosive surge. She grabbed him and screamed softly in his ear.

After four whiskeys, Willie began to feel a bit boisterous, sort of craving action. He had been riding hard, thinking hard, and now he wanted a bit of fun to get the devil out of his system.

First to business. He had been looking sharp at the hard-faced characters drinking at the round bar. It didn't take more than a minute's scrutiny to pick his man. He had a lot of judgment in such matters. A roustabout in a short black bowler, blotchy face, stubble-bearded, with a worn rusty shirt.

"Joady," Willie said, and stood up. Joady, recognizing the note in his voice, followed Willie to the round bar. They stopped about ten feet from the man in the bowler.

"What's up, Willie?" Joady asked.

"Look, Deadeye's a good man, but a knothead. We gotta protect him."

"A backup?" said Joady, who knew something about how his brother's mind worked.

"Right. That brawler in the bowler. Looks like the right man. He'd shoot his grandfather for a bottle of booze. Give him twenty-five dollars and tell him there's the same after he does the job." Willie pulled bills from his pocket and put them in Joady's fist. "Tell him to go slow on the whiskey till the job's done."

"What's the setup, Willie?"

Willie had worked out the plan. "Easy. Slocum comes ridin' in, heads for the saloon to either find us or find out about us. He's gutsy and thinks he's a hot gun. So he rides in straight up. He gets off his horse. Who's waitin'? Deadeye at the railpost, and up on the roof, cross the street, set this brawler with a gun. You know the rest. Deadeye bumps Slocum, passes a coupla insults, and Deadeye pulls his gun. If Deadeye is slow, the brawler will hit Slocum."

Joady nodded. "You're one devil, Willie. I tole you, you're makin' Slocum bigger than he is."

"Mebbe," said Willie. "But it's better to be on the safe side. We got a lot of money, Joady, and I'd like to be around to spend it."

Joady shrugged and growled. "I hate that Slocum's guts, and I'm gonna feel cheated if I can't get a bullet in him."

"What the hell does it matter how he goes, Joady? Why stick your neck out. We got Deadeye and a gun for hire. Let them do the dirty work. The idea, Joady, is to live fast and easy, not to go round provin' you're the fastest gun. 'Cause there ain't no such gun." He brushed his nose and stared at the hard-face in the bowler hat. "Now go over and put the money in his hand. He'll do it." Then Willie motioned to Saunders, who came over to pour him another whiskey.

At the table, Deadeye watched Willie and Joady talking at the bar, then looked at a saloon girl with a painted face and skimpy skirt drifting about at the far end of the saloon. She was unsteady and didn't see Deadeye, which displeased him. He got up, nodded to Ketchum and Belle, and walked to the woman.

Ketchum grinned. "Deadeye never gets tired of women."

"Do you, Ketch?" Belle asked.

He shrugged and looked at her. "I s'pose there are some women a man could never get tired of."

Belle's blue eyes looked stony. "I fear I ain't one of them. Looks like Joady's tired of me."

Ketchum shook his head. "Joady is the biggest fool ever came to birth. Never stuck to anyone or anything. If he didn't have Willie takin' care of him, he'd be long gone."

She sighed. "I confess I'm a touch disappointed in Joady."

Ketch grimaced. "He don't know how to treat a fine lady, as I tole him."

"That how you think of me, Ketch?"

"That's how." He gazed at Belle with honest admiration.

She drew a heavy sigh. "Sure hate it that I didn't see you the better man, Ketch. Sorry I gave myself to him. I got a feeling he don't care any more what happens to me."

"Reckon it's smart for you to think that, little lady. Joady never thinks more than what he wants right now."

Belle looked thoughtful, then said, "What's Willie gonna do when Diana catches up?"

"No knowin' exactly what Willie will do," Ketch said, raising his glass.

"Will he hurt her?" Belle's eyes shone anxiously.

Ketchum smiled grimly. "She's a dead shot and she's shootin' at him. He's gonna protect himself. Willie does that, always."

She glanced at Willie at the bar, his face concentrated in thought. "Sometimes Willie gives me the shivers."

Ketchum laughed. "Gives me the shivers, too. And he's my cousin."

"I sure hope he won't hurt Diana," she said.

Ketch looked toward the smoky bar where the men stood close, laughing and talking. Willie was looking at him, and started toward the table.

"I think Willie wants to stop Slocum," Ketch said. "Once that's done, he figgers he'll handle Diana all right."

Willie stomped to the table, slouched in his chair, and watched Joady talking to the roustabout. His blotchy face looked at the money Joady put in his fist and he grinned. It looked like a deal.

Willie glanced about. "Deadeye's with the whores, as usual." He looked at Ketch with narrowed eyes, then lit a cigarillo. "You might scout east a bit, Ketch. Mebbe we'll get an idea when Slocum's gonna hit town."

Ketch didn't like it. There was no need to worry, but he felt a sense of unease in leaving Belle. Still, it was a sensible idea to scout and stay ahead of Slocum.

He got up, glanced at Belle, and the sudden look in her eyes jarred him. He couldn't figure it, and was still puzzling about it when he pushed through the bat-wing doors of the saloon and walked to railpost where his horse was tied. He looked at the full moon spilling light on the town street. As he swung over the saddle he was hit again by the strange look in Belle's eyes. What was she trying to tell him? he wondered as the horse jogged along.

• • •

Willie looked with pleasure at Belle's fresh young face,
her beautiful violet-blue eyes, her bust, and the itch came
over him. He had a lot of whiskey in him, and felt in
the mood.

He picked up her hand. "Don't like the way Joady
treats you, honey."

She looked at his bronzed, broad-boned face. "Don't
like it much myself, Willie."

"Tell you what. From now on you can forget about
Joady."

Her brow furrowed and she looked at his big coarse
hand holding her small delicate one. "What d'you mean,
Willie?"

He smiled. "Let's go upstairs for a bit of privacy. Tell
you there what I mean."

She stared at him. Her premonitions were coming true.
She'd fallen for Joady, who turned out to be a polecat.
It should have been Ketch all along. Now Willie was
pushing. And the idea of Willie hit her like a sack of
stones.

"What you got in mind upstairs?"

He grinned broadly. "Guess you're gonna hafta go up
to find out."

Her eyes narrowed. "I got a notion what you got in
mind, Willie."

His smile spread. "You're a smart filly."

She pointed to one of the saloon girls. "You got an
itch, Willie? Whyn't you use her?"

His face hardened. "Don't want a worn-out saloon
hussy." He smiled. "You're fresh as a daisy, honey. Ain't
knocked around saloons. You're what I want, Belle."

"How 'bout Joady? He won't like this."

Willie shrugged. "He won't mind. We're brothers, we share."

"What about me? S'pose I don't like it? Being disloyal to Joady."

"But I'm tellin' you, Belle, he don't care. Now be a good little girl and don't make me mean."

"S'pose I don't want to go upstairs, Willie?"

He looked startled, then the icy look hit his eyes that she had seen before. His face screwed with thought. "Diana is comin' with Slocum. I got plans for Slocum. And I figure once he's outa the way, I'll be able to get some reason into Diana. But I might jest change my mind and get a bullet in Diana. Takes care of a lot of trouble."

Belle looked at the cold gray eyes of Willie James, outlaw, killer, and robber.

"Are you tellin' me you'd shoot Diana, just because I might decline your attentions, Willie?"

His voice sounded dead. "Reckon I'm tellin' you that."

"You're a mangy dog, Willie James. Guess I got no choice."

"No choice," he said, and pointed to the stairs.

Ketchum rode east in the night, looking for riders, looking at the deep shadows of the massive canyon glittering in the moonlight, but he saw nothing of Slocum. His mind, however, was not on Slocum.

Suddenly Ketch went hard-jawed, pulled hard on the reins, turned the horse, and started back to town. He finally understood that look in Belle's eyes. It was an appeal for help. But why? Who did she fear? Willie?

Couldn't be Joady, nor Deadeye. Ketch spurred his horse. She had sent him a signal for help, that was clear. Willie was in his whiskey mood, and loosened up, he did funny things. But would Willie go for Belle? He was in the whiskey, and whiskey Willie could be lusty, a mean, wild-running stallion.

Ketch reached the saloon, came off the horse on the run, flung the reins around the railpost. He pushed open the doors, walked into the smoky saloon, pushed past the men at the bar. He looked at the table. Deadeye and a saloon hussy were sitting there sipping whiskey. Ketch's eyes swept the saloon. No sign of Willie or Belle. He saw Joady at the bar talking with the brawler. There was a leaden feeling in Ketch's gut.

He moved in front of Deadeye. "Where's Willie?"

"Did ya spot Slocum?" Deadeye asked.

"Where's Willie?"

With a wolfish leer, Deadeye jerked his thumb at the rooms upstairs.

Ketchum felt a surge of rage. That blasted Willie had sent him on a wild-goose chase, just so he could push the kid. It was damned rotten. Ketch suddenly found himself on the stairs, his heart pounding. He felt he was doing something crazy, but he couldn't stop. He listened carefully at two doors, then turned the knob of one and walked in.

Belle was nude, sitting on the bed, and Willie, clothed, with his Levi's unbuttoned, his organ out, was standing in front of her.

"Jesus," said Willie.

Ketch looked at Belle. Her eyes were pleading. She didn't want any part of it.

Ketch pulled his gun. "What's goin' on?"

Willie stared at him. "Gone loco, Ketch?"

Ketch drew a deep breath. "Is this what you want, Belle?"

"To be honest, Ketch..." Her eyes spoke volumes.

Ketch's mouth was a hard line. "I'm sorry, Willie. I like the kid. And she doesn't want this. We ain't gonna force her, are we?"

Willie smiled brilliantly. "'Course not, Ketch. There's twenty out there like her. She don't mean a thing. On your way down, Ketch, send up a good-lookin' slut." He grinned. "They're all the same, Ketch. Some day you'll learn."

Ketch's eyes were chilly. "Don't believe that, Willie. And I'm sorry 'bout this. No hard feelin's?"

"Naw. One's jest like another, I tole you."

Ketch looked at Belle's lovely face, at her white shapely body. He bit his lip. He really cared for the kid.

"Get dressed," he said.

She slipped into her clothing while Willie buttoned up, pulled out a cigarillo, and lit it, sitting on the bed.

Now dressed, Belle came closer to Ketch. "I'm sorry, Willie," Ketch said, moving his gun toward his holster.

Willie's hand was fast; his gun barked, and a red splotch burst on Ketchum's forehead as he stumbled back.

Belle screamed.

There was silence.

Willie walked over to look down at Ketchum, then said, "Didn't mind him wantin' you, Belle, but he never shoulda pulled a gun on me. Now you jest be quiet. He's got a gun in his hand. I'll tell Joady he was jealous and tried for a showdown. That's what you saw. Jest remember that, Belle. Now, let's go quiet out that door. I'll get Saunders to give Ketch a nice place in Boot Hill."

As they went through the door, Willie cursed softly. "Damn Ketch. He never did tell me when Slocum would be ridin' in."

# 12

Slocum had been reconnoitering a way to come safely into Tombstone when he saw the lone horseman. In the full moonlight, he looked to Slocum's sharp eyes like Ketchum. Rifle in hand, Slocum eased off the roan, and slipped behind a boulder. He remembered Ketchum, the one who'd said, "hold it, we might be hanging the wrong man."

Ketchum seemed to be looking at tracks, then his gaze swept the canyon. Suddenly he pulled hard at the reins and wheeled his horse back toward town, riding at a gallop.

Found something? What in hell could he find? Nothing. But he sure went into a hard run toward Tombstone. Slocum came from behind the boulder, rubbing his chin thoughtfully. Ketchum was out here trying to get a sniff on him and Diana. That had to be it. It meant Willie was in Tombstone, waiting. What would he do? He'd set up an ambush, that's what.

Slocum's face was grim as he rode back to the cache where he'd left Diana. She had everything packed in the saddlebags. She looked at him.

"Saw Ketchum," he said. "Scoutin' for us, I'd say."

Her face hardened. "Then they're waitin'."

"And we're comin'. We ride in north to hit the saloon. We come in soft, so if Willie has set up anything, we'll spot it."

In the quiet of the silver night, they rode half a mile north, then cantered toward the lights of the town. In the bright moonlight, Slocum could see the bulking frame houses with their lamplight, and could hear sounds. Laughing, shouts of drunks, a wide-open town where the gun was your best friend.

They swung off the horses, tied them to a bush, and walked softly forward. The bright moonlight seemed to etch everything sharply. Good for ambush, Slocum thought, but good for them, too.

The space between the big saloon and the livery next to it was about six yards, and Slocum moved softly for it. He thought about Willie and Joady, who had tried to lynch him for no reason at all. He thought of Biggers and Snouts, of Burt and his gang—all mean, mangy dogs who spoiled the life. They had grabbed Belle, an innocent kid, and who knew how they abused her. The world might be a pleasant place to live if you could only get rid of the wolves who preyed on innocent folk.

Thinking like this put him in an icy rage by the time he got into the space between the saloon and the livery.

Now he could see the street, cowboys laughing and

drunk. Five men loafed in front of the saloon, innocent enough. He studied them. He had an eye for the outlaw. One man caught his attention, narrow-faced, drooping mustache, short-brimmed hat. He was smoking, and his eyes squinted at the east side of town. What was he looking for? He was waiting, that was sure. For who? And Willie's bunch, where were they? Holed up. It'd be smart for Willie to put out this hombre for ambush, a strange face, not anyone Slocum would expect. And if Willie's bunch lay low, Slocum was supposed to think they had gone hotfoot out of Tombstone. So, what was the setup? Just this hombre? One man? Didn't seem smart, and Willie was smart.

He turned to Diana, crouched ten yards from him, and pointed to the man in the narrow hat. "Watch him, where he looks. He might be in Willie's bunch," Slocum said softly.

She nodded and her eyes riveted on the man. "Let me go first, and get behind him." She pulled her hat down over her face.

He frowned, not liking that, but she'd already started, walking slowly, moving out in the street.

The man, and it was Deadeye, had just glanced at the saloon, and when he turned it startled him to see her. He stiffened, bent his knees, his hand ready, then caught himself. He looked past her, but saw nothing. It puzzled him. Then Deadeye caught a movement on the roof across the street, moonlight gleaming off a gun.

*Backup!* Deadeye was angry, but to hell with it. He didn't want a backup, but Willie was Willie, taking no chances. Anyway, Deadeye felt he'd get the first bullet in Slocum, just to prove who was the better man. Where

the hell was he? That had to be Diana. She looked like
the older sister of Belle, a good-looking filly. After he
knocked off Slocum, she might want to lean on him.
Women did that sort of thing, gave themselves to the
better man.

Though these ideas went through his mind, Deadeye
never relaxed, but kept his eyes moving restlessly. And
sure enough, there was his man, Slocum, appearing like
magic, out of the shadows. He was big, all right, but
moved catlike; he looked hard, tough, big-chested; the
light caught his piercing eyes that seemed to drill through
Deadeye. Did he know something? Did he know this was
a setup? How could he? A dangerous man, but he could
be caught off guard. And it didn't matter that he looked
tough. A bullet took them all down.

He was close now, glancing at the saloon doors. Looking for Willie?

Deadeye made his move as if drunk, staggered hard
into Slocum. Damn, the man was rock-hard.

"Whyn't hell don't you look where yuh goin', you
drunken polecat!" Deadeye's voice was harsh, insulting.

Slocum moved to face him and the saloon doors. "I
think you bumped me, mister," Slocum said. "And you
should be right careful 'bout your language."

A cool bastard, Deadeye thought, but he'll be dead
in a minute. "A mangy drunk always thinks it's the other
hombre," he said, crouching a bit, hands at his side.
"And you got a blasted nerve talkin' like that. I don't
like the look of you. Remind me of a buzzard I once had
to shoot."

That did it.

There was a frozen moment.

The men loafing in front of the saloon were watching, petrified.

The sound of four guns blasted the night.

Deadeye's gun was out; he had fired, but his bullet went wild. His chest was shattered by Slocum's bullet and blood was pumping out as he sank to the ground.

Slocum, crouching, had swung around, looking for ambush. A man in a rusty shirt, on the roof, across the street, had been hit, and had somersaulted to the ground; he was lying face down, gun in hand.

Slocum looked at Diana. Her gun was still out.

"I saw him up there, leaning out, aiming," she said. "The moon shone on the barrel of his gun."

"Thanks," Slocum said. He looked grim-faced at the dead man in front of him. Just another body. Willie was still sending men out to catch the bullet meant for him.

Slocum shot a glance at the saloon doors. Would Willie be in there waiting, in case he survived the ambush? Or did Willie just post his hired gun out here to do the dirty work and hoof out with the money and the bunch?

The men on the porch pushed against the wall as Slocum, gun in hand, moved catlike, easing open one batwing door and peering in. No Willie. He glanced at the stairs.

"Wait here, Diana," he whispered. He slipped into the saloon, hugging the walls, went noiselessly up the stairs, kicked open one door after the other. He saw Ketchum sprawled bloody on the floor, dead of a bullet in the head.

Then he heard horses galloping hard. He hurried to the window. The three of them, Willie, Joady, and Belle, were racing out of Tombstone; too far and too dark for a decent shot. He watched them, and instead of turning southwest at the end of town, they rode straight west, the trail to White Gulch, which could be a mistake.

Slocum knew White Gulch, hot as an inferno at midday, bleak and deadly at night. Willie could be bottled up there, blocked by the face of the massive canyon, if he made the decision to ride there.

Slocum went down, still holding his gun. The men were watching him, and Diana was chafing, already on her horse. "They're not that far ahead. Let's stick, let's not give 'em breathing space," she said.

They rode hard for a time, but Willie managed to stay in front, riding hard west. He was headed for White Gulch, all right, a blister of a place, as Slocum remembered, tricky with crags, boulders, and hideaways. Willie wasn't all that dumb, after all. True, his back would be to the wall, but it was tricky country, good for ambush. Now the moon was swinging behind a gathering of clouds. When Slocum found good boulder cover, he pulled his reins.

"Why are we stopping?" she demanded. "I'm sick of everyone getting killed but Willie."

"So am I, but we'll spend the night here, Diana. We'll need the light. Tomorrow it's showdown with Willie. He's got a great stone canyon at his back, nowhere to go."

Her eyes gleamed. "The final trap."

"Sorta," he said, thinking of ambush, and that the trap could go both ways.

After he took care of the horses and they had settled

down, Slocum finally said, "Ketchum's dead. Saw him in the upstairs room."

She looked startled. "The one good man in the bunch. I liked him." After a moment's thought, she said, "Fight over Belle, I suppose?"

"Good guess. Joady or Willie did it. They've got no loyalties. Kill their own."

"Ketch liked Belle," she said dolefully. "Do you think he was tryin' to protect her?"

"I reckon."

She stared at the dark blue clouds shot through with moonlight, then at the stark, desolate look of the canyon, a great immensity of rock, grotesque with shadows. "Figger we're gonna snare them tomorrow, Slocum?"

"Yeah. They've got nowhere to go. Back against the wall. It's gotta be showdown time."

Slocum put his hands behind his head, looked at the moon which suddenly broke out of the clouds and shone like pure silver against the deep blue sky. Then his gaze went down to the forlorn landscape of the canyon, and the bizarre shadows of its crags and peaks.

Slocum felt a curious gust of feeling. Against these massive canyons, man seemed such a puny creature.

He thought of the ageless time of the canyons and the short life of men. This time tomorrow either he or Willie would be dead.

And if Willie was smarter or luckier, it might be him looking at the great canyons.

Slocum didn't like the feeling and twisted restlessly on his bedroll. Diana was lying nearby, the moon rays slanting off the fine bones of her face, the roundness of her breasts. She was a woman, and somehow her body held warmth against the idea of death. He moved to her. Her eyes were open, deep brown pools, full of feelings. Did she sense his thoughts. Suddenly she opened her arms to him.

He held her close, kissed her full, warm lips. It was not only passion, but the feeling of one human being connected to another in a dangerous world. The moon and the stars flung their light on the eternal canyons.

They made love and it had something special, and when the climax came, Slocum felt the most intense pleasure. Still, he slept uneasy, his mind sifting the sounds of the night for danger.

Next morning his eyes opened to a great orange sun rising in a drained sky. He looked down the trail as it twisted toward the valley. Last night the moon shadows had made weird shapes, but now it was dazzling with white sand, spiky cactus, thick brush, boulders, and behind them, rising steeply, the massive walls of the canyon.

Slocum's green eyes swept the valley. The sun seemed to have bleached everything, the bones of animals, even the rocks. By noon White Gulch might turn into a frying pan. Somewhere down there Willie lurked, gun ready, waiting for him to make one mistake.

Slocum poured water into his hat and let the horses drink. As the sun began to climb, they started to ride the twisting trail down. The prints were clear, three horses moving at a good clip into the gulch. Slocum studied every rock, brush, crevice, whatever Willie could use as an ambush site.

It didn't take long for Slocum to appreciate how well

Willie had picked his ground. His trail went through the maze of boulders and dry brush. Slocum never let his concentration falter. Lower and lower they rode toward the floor of the valley, and only once did Slocum dare to glance back toward their starting point.

He looked at Diana; her face was flushed from the heat, and tight-lipped with determination. *Plenty of guts,* he thought admiringly.

A sharp twist in the trail made him fiercely alert; the land was pocked with boulders and crevices, places to hide, to shoot from.

He dared not turn his head, but made a warning gesture to Diana. When they came to another twist in the trail, he cursed softly.

There was Belle, lying face down on the earth, her arms tied beneath her body. She lay like a stone.

At the sight, Diana let out a sharp cry, jumped from her horse, running forward.

Slocum's nerves tingled, and he, too, slipped off his saddle, crouching, his gun out, his eyes searching the nearby rocks and bushes. When Diana reached Belle, she cried, "Honey, what have they done!" When she turned Belle over, Diana's eyes shocked wide. She was looking into a pointed gun.

"Have you gone loco, Belle?"

Belle glanced at Slocum, who threw himself to the ground near a boulder, ready to shoot the gun from Belle's hand, when a shot from nearby boulders whistled past him, forcing him to scramble for the red boulder.

Belle came to her feet, her pistol still pointing to Diana. "Had to do it, Diana," she said. "They've got a gun on me. They'll kill me if I don't. But it'll be all right. Willie just wants to talk, not to hurt you. It's Slocum they're after."

Diana glared. "You must be crazy. I'll never go near Willie."

"Joady has me under his gun right now," Belle said grimly. "He'll shoot if you don't come with me."

Diana stared in hopeless fury. Willie with his killer instinct had stacked the cards, used Belle again to get the edge. He fought dirty every time.

What should she do, what could she do? She didn't want to pull back from Slocum, but Willie said he'd kill Belle. Could she take the chance he was bluffing? He carried big money, and he wasn't going to let it get away.

"Gimme your gun, Diana."

"No, won't do it. Won't give up my gun."

Willie, who had been listening from behind the big white rectangular rocks called out, "It's all right, Belle, she can keep her gun as long as she comes with you. Is it a deal, Diana?"

"Maybe," Diana said after a long moment, hating his voice, hating Willie, and hoping that once she got near him, she'd find a time to put a bullet in him.

Willie's voice grated with satisfaction. "Hear that, Slocum? Your goose is cooked."

Slocum didn't bother to answer. He was studying the land behind him, thinking that he had a precious minute to make a move.

"Hey, Slocum, you shoulda stayed in Tombstone," Joady crowed. "We coulda buried you there with honors, made you a legend."

Diana stood up next to Belle, still hesitating. And

Willie, aware of that, called out. "We gotcha covered, Diana. I promise you there'll be no hurtin'. Just want to reason with you. Even give your money back. It's your lawful wedded husband Willie James talkin' at you."

Slocum, peering at Diana, suddenly saw her chin harden. She'd made the decision to go with Belle; he could read it. He had to be ready.

"D'ye mean what you're sayin', Willie James? 'Bout the money? Or is this another of your tricks?"

"Yeah, honey, I mean it. We got a big haul from the bank at Tucson. Don't need your money no more. Glad to give it back. Glad to get you off my tail. C'mon over and we'll talk."

Diana threw a strange look in the direction of Slocum, then said to Belle, "Let's go."

Slocum crawled from one side of the boulder to the other, and from the bottom watched Diana and Belle walking toward the big white rectangular rocks, then disappear behind them.

Lightning-quick he crawled swiftly back on his elbows, under brush to the boulder to the left behind him. Flat as a pancake, he scrambled again, to another boulder.

From here he might be able to navigate. Then he stopped to think. They would talk, and Willie might give Diana her money, which might take the steam out of her. Did she still have strong feelings about Willie? What would happen when she got close to him? Would she forget the hate, would old tender feelings awaken? Willie might put his arm around her, hold her tight, and, like a woman, she might forgive what he had done to her.

Slocum rubbed his chin. Where would that leave him

but with his gun and his wits?

He studied the ground near him, thick with brush and boulder. His jaw clenched.

When the sisters reached Willie's position behind the rectangular boulders, he gave Diana a broad grin. "Well, Diana, honey, it's good to see you again. Nobody's gonna shoot you, sweetie. We had too many good times. Remember?"

She glared at him. There he stood, the man she probably hated more than anyone, yet she couldn't whip out her gun and shoot him, the thing she had craved to do from the moment he ran from her bed and stole her money. He was still handsome, with powerful shoulders, a broad, bronzed face, and those shrewd, secretive gray eyes. Crazy feelings stirred her: anger that he'd left her, that he'd stolen her money, grabbed young Belle. And the feelings that came during the night when, as his wife, she lay in his arms. Could she shoot him in cold blood? Shoot him at all? He had done rotten things and he deserved to die like a dog, but could she do it?

"Don't sweet-talk me, Willie James. Did you mean that 'bout my money?"

He had been watching her like a hawk, as if he could read her thoughts, and would know if she was going to try for her gun. Now his gray eyes glinted with humor. "Sorry I took the money. To tell you the truth, Diana, I was just takin' it as a stake. Aimed to return it. Didn't I say that, Joady? Made a heavy haul in Tucson. Don't need your money. Right, Joady?"

Joady, squinting out from behind the boulder, nodded. "I swear he did, Diana. Last thing he wanted to do. He tole me, it was more like a loan."

"In that case," Diana said, "just give it back. Now."

Willie nodded and pointed to his horse. "Tied in the saddlebag for safekeeping. We don't want to put time on that. Not till we get Slocum off our backs." He pulled out a cigarillo and lit it. "No point in having money if someone out there ain't gonna let you have time to spend it, right?"

Diana's brown eyes gazed at him, and Willie couldn't tell what she was thinking. But it didn't matter. In his mind, he had canceled her gun. He and Joady now had the edge, for they just had to face Slocum's gun. He looked approvingly at Joady, who kept his eye peeled, watching the red boulder, Slocum's position.

"Has he moved?" Willie demanded.

"Not an inch."

"Don't take your eye off that red boulder, not for anything," Willie growled.

Joady's smile was sinister. "All I need is just a piece of him to show." Then he stared at Diana. "Better get her gun, Willie. Can't feel easy on my back while she's got it."

Willie smiled, but his gray eyes were cold. "Nothin' to worry 'bout, Joady. Diana's a good girl, smart. She won't do anything stupid. But we don't want to worry Joady, Diana. So you'd better gimme your gun, honey. We don't want you hurt."

"Nobody gets my gun," she said, hard-faced.

Willie studied her, and didn't like what he was seeing. He glanced at Joady. "Has he made a move? Not like him to jest wait."

"Hasn't moved an inch, I swear, Willie. Never took

my eye off that rock. Mebbe he's knocked out that Diana took a walk."

"Mebbe yes, mebbe no," Willie said, perplexed by Diana's mulishness. "C'mon, honey, be nice. Tell yuh what. S'posin' I give you your money. Would you gimme the gun?"

"Might be," she said, tight-lipped. "Let's try it."

He grinned. "You're slick, Diana. It's one thing I always liked 'bout you. All right. We'll do that." Crouched low, he moved to the saddlebag of his horse, reached into it, and pulled out a bulky leather pouch. He came back and held it out.

She studied him hard, stepped back. "Willie, I got no reason yet to trust you. Toss it over."

A crafty gleam appeared in his gray eyes, and he grinned. "Got an honest heart, honey, where you're concerned." He tossed the bag at her, and she caught it deftly.

"Didn't think you'd do that," she said.

"Now throw your gun, honey."

She studied him, and what she sensed deep in his eyes firmed her jaw. "Nope. I feel safer with it, Willie James."

Joady turned and glared. "Willie. Don't want that woman with a gun while my back is to her, you hear me?"

Willie's face hardened. "Gimme the gun, Diana. Ain't gonna ask you another time."

"Tole you, Willie, I feel safer with it."

Joady shot Willie a hard glance and his mouth twisted viciously. Willie's face now lost all its charm; it had become menacing. "I'm sick o' you, Diana. I'm gonna tell you now, because you ain't got a chance in hell comin' here. You ain't gettin' out of this alive. I'm not only gonna take your gun, but your money. Jest playin' a game with you, 'cause we like Belle. She's our kinda woman. For her sake, we gave you a chance."

"You'd shoot a woman, Willie James?" she asked quickly.

His gray eyes gleamed viciously. "Won't be the first time. Now, gimme your gun or you're dead quick."

Only Joady heard the soft scrape of the stone ten feet to the left of their position. Startled, he looked out, then because of a sudden intuition that somehow Slocum had got away from that red boulder, he started to scramble.

At the same time, Diana, her eyes rooted on Willie, seeing her own death in his eyes, went for her gun.

Willie's hand flashed to his holster, and he was bringing his gun up when Slocum's bullet crashed into his right shoulder. The gun dropped from Willie's paralyzed hand and he pitched back. Diana and Belle looked astonished at Slocum, who had worked his way in a circle behind Willie's position.

Willie stared viciously at Slocum. "The devil himself," he muttered.

"Joady?" Slocum asked Diana.

She shook her head, bewildered. "Dunno. He was just here."

Slocum, keeping an eye on Willie, eased over to look out, but could see only boulders, the brush, and the hot sand of the valley.

Willie was smiling at Slocum. "You're a hard man to beat, Slocum."

"And you're a hard man to catch, Willie, but you're gonna hang."

"A man's gotta go, one way or another," Willie said

with a smile. He was thinking about Joady; the game wasn't over yet.

"Look, Slocum, I got 'bout twenty thousand in new money in that saddlebag. All yours. Jest take it, take the women, and go."

Slocum's face was grim. "You got a date with a rope, Willie."

"Don't like money?" He held his shoulder and glanced down at the gun, still near him. "Tell me this, Slocum; I gotta know. Did you ever meet up with a man named Burt?"

Slocum's piercing green eyes studied Willie lying there.

"Yeah, we met Burt and your boys outside Tucson. They ain't movin' much."

"It's what I figgered," said Willie wearily, his eyes slitted. Yes, he had wanted to know about Burt, but mostly he was working to give Joady time. He saw movement behind Slocum. Joady! A moment more and then they'd blast Slocum to hell, and with him these miserable women who'd been a curse to the bunch.

"Slocum!" cried Diana.

Joady had made a silent circle, his heart pounding with hate. How he hated that Slocum, who had never stopped tracking them, like some devil-obsessed lion. But this was the time he'd rip that bastard apart. He had felt terrible fear that Willie was gone, but now could hear his voice calmly talking to Slocum. Willie was giving him time. They had played this game before. Now he had reached the thick brush. If he made a run, he'd come in behind Slocum; could anything be sweeter? He could almost see Belle and Diana. Willie on the ground would sense he was coming, and would be smart. Damn, a diversion to let him get in there noiselessly and blast Slocum to hell. Maybe force him to drop his gun, then shoot him to pieces, a little at a time. He took a deep breath, started forward, and in that instant, Willie's left hand grabbed his gun. He was raising it to shoot when Slocum's bullet crashed into his chest. And Joady, rushing for the clear shot at Slocum, never pulled his trigger. The front part of his head blossomed with blood.

A bullet from Belle's gun did it.

Slocum looked at the grave he had dug, then at the marker for it. Using his bowie knife, he had smoothed the wood and then printed words on it in pencil. He set the marker at the head of the grave.

Diana crouched down to read the words:

*HERE LIES WILLIE JAMES AND HIS BROTHER, JOADY. THEY ROBBED AND KILLED THEIR WAY OVER KANSAS, TEXAS, AND THE ARIZONA TERRITORY. THEIR EVIL WAYS CAUGHT UP WITH THEM IN WHITE GULCH. IT WAS A PLEASURE TO BURY THEM HERE.*
                              *Signed—John Slocum*

"They sure got their just desserts," Belle said.

Diana looked at her. "I thought you were crazy 'bout Joady."

"I musta been crazy all right," Belle said. "A rotten polecat. I knew he'd be comin' back after Slocum. I was prayin' he'd come. And I jest waited. Only sorry he didn't know it was my bullet."

Slocum smiled. "Thank you, Belle. You're a dead

shot, too. Like Diana. Runs in the family."

Diana watched him walk to his roan.

"Why don't you come to the ranch with us for a spell, Slocum?" she said. "It's a fine spread. Promise you a great time."

Slocum's eyebrows knitted; he thought of Diana's beautiful body.

"Can't resist a promise like that, Diana," he said.

They laughed, swung over their saddles, and started up the trail.

The sun began to broil White Gulch, and by mid-afternoon, it practically turned into a frying pan.

# JAKE LOGAN

# GREAT WESTERN YARNS FROM ONE OF THE BEST-SELLING WRITERS IN THE FIELD TODAY

# JAKE LOGAN

| | | |
|---|---|---|
| ___ 0-867-21003 | BLOODY TRAIL TO TEXAS | $1.95 |
| ___ 0-867-21041 | THE COMANCHE'S WOMAN | $1.95 |
| ___ 0-872-16979 | OUTLAW BLOOD | $1.95 |
| ___ 06191-4 | THE CANYON BUNCH | $2.25 |
| ___ 06255-4 | SLOCUM'S JUSTICE | $2.25 |
| ___ 05958-8 | SLOCUM'S RAID | $1.95 |
| ___ 06481-6 | SWAMP FOXES | $2.25 |
| ___ 0-872-16823 | SLOCUM'S CODE | $1.95 |
| ___ 0-867-21071 | SLOCUM'S DEBT | $1.95 |
| ___ 0-867-21090 | SLOCUM'S GOLD | $1.95 |
| ___ 0-867-21023 | SLOCUM'S HELL | $1.95 |
| ___ 0-867-21087 | SLOCUM'S REVENGE | $1.95 |
| ___ 06413-1 | SLOCUM GETS EVEN | $2.50 |
| ___ 06744-0 | SLOCUM AND THE LOST DUTCHMAN MINE | $2.50 |